VIRAL
EVOLUTION

MD JOBE

ISBN: 978-1-963569-34-6 hard cover
ISBN: 978-1-963569-35-3 soft cover

Edited by: Melissa Long

Warren publishing

Published by Warren Publishing
Charlotte, NC
www.warrenpublishing.net
Printed in the United States

*For my wife and family, whose love and support
have given me the motivation to tell my story.*

PROLOGUE

The headlights try in vain to pierce the dense fog of the South American jungle. Objects appear suddenly only to vanish again, fading into the mist. The Jeep bounces and bucks as it leaps over the jungle's natural speed bumps.

"How can you see in this crazy fog?" the passenger, José, asks in a heavy Spanish accent as he clings to the roll bars, his veins bulging through his meaty forearms. He shifts his weight back and forth, trying to not get thrown into the brush.

The driver remains silent, concentrating on the task at hand. He then confidently pulls the Jeep into a clearing.

The area is about thirty yards long and ten yards wide. The floor is a mess of matted-down branches and brush, as if a golfing divot was taken out of the dense tree cover. It is a few minutes before dusk, and the shadows of the jungle are creeping across the worksite. A group of three men are working, huddled around a tripod drilling machine twenty yards out into the clearing. One short and plump man with his sweat-soaked shirt flopping over his belly is handling a control panel. A taller man, with a spotty, brown beard and sweaty wisps of a comb-over plastered to his head, is taking notes in a flimsy binder. All the while, the third man, younger and stoutly built, is holding the sides of the tripod to steady it. The hot, steamy mist floats along the ground, covering everything in a dew-like coating.

The men stop working as the Jeep's engine comes to a halt. One of the men, who had been tending to the control panel, approaches the Jeep, his face awash with sweat and dirt. "I see you didn't get lost on your recon mission," he rasps, wiping a hint of dirt off his brow with the end of his ragged shirtsleeve.

The driver, known only to the men as Mr. Vincent, and his hired assistant, José, ease down from the Jeep. José is carrying an AK-47 leisurely strung over his right shoulder, like a ladies' swag bag.

"We did a five-mile sweep of the surrounding area, Dr. Shaw. It appears that we are alone. Have you made any progress in our absence?" replies Mr. Vincent coldly.

"Well, I have good news and bad news for you," says Shaw with a hint of a smug grin. "The good news is that we have finally come up with a sample that is clear of the radiation signatures that have haunted us this entire expedition. The ore samples are clean and about two hundred feet below the jungle floor. A very attainable distance. Again, much better than our first eight locations."

"And the bad news?" Mr. Vincent inquires, waiting for a response he has already anticipated.

The other two scientists have stopped working and are walking up on either side of Dr. Shaw. Dr. Knowles, the taller of the two, interrupts and states rather matter-of-factly while crossing his arms across his thin chest, "We are not in the same country. You idiots took us over the border. I was able to figure it out as I set up the GPS locator to mark the location of the sample draw." He quickly thumbs back through his binder, locating his exact notes on the location.

"We are at least fifteen miles into Colombia by our estimation," continues Shaw, waving his hand dismissively at the binder. "I am pretty sure our contracts do not extend outside Ecuador."

"What that means is that all this work and all of our findings are for nothing!" Dr. Knowles blurts out, raising his voice and causing a rustling in the jungle surrounding them. "Only the radiated metal that we found in our previous samplings was in the country we are working with. The one sample that we have found without radiation, our one success, is over the damn border!" He throws up his arms and stomps around in a small circle, like a spoiled child. "I am hot and wet and pissed off," he rants, frustratedly pulling at his shirt. Pointing his finger suddenly at Mr. Vincent, he scolds, "*You* are supposed to be able to navigate this jungle and protect us from rogue rebel parties, not take us out of Ecuador to the place where these groups run free. We are in real danger here, not to mention our findings are crap."

A thin smile creeps across José's face, forming a tooth-decayed grin.

Mr. Vincent remains calm. "We just completed a recon sweep, and we are alone and safe. Your findings are as expected. We are done here." Mr. Vincent turns toward the Jeep, making eye contact with José.

"What do you mean 'as expected'?" Dr. Knowles exclaims, his arms rising to the heavens.

José shifts the AK-47 under his arm and lights up the jungle mist with a barrage of gunfire. The three scientists are instantly sliced to ribbons at such a close distance.

"Well done, José," says Mr. Vincent, standing at the driver's side door. "Time to go."

He then pulls out his sidearm and shoots José three times in the chest. "It appears Dr. Knowles was right," he says as José's corpse crumples to the ground. "This is a dangerous area. Rebels like you, José, could rob or kill anyone for no reason at all." He climbs behind the wheel of the Jeep and retrieves his satellite phone from the middle console.

After two rings, the line is picked up and a sleepy voice asks, "How is the progress?"

"I have the samples and am heading back," Mr. Vincent says.

"Send the samples to our Madison contact for testing. Stay in Ecuador for a few days to clean up any confusion about what may have happened."

"Yes, sir," replies Mr. Vincent before hanging up and disappearing in the mist.

CHAPTER 1

Decklan Thomas cringes at the smell of snuffed-out cigarettes and cheap beer on his clothes. Somehow all college after-parties smell like stale hops and brats. It is a pungent aroma, even over that of his own distillery-scented body.

As he drags himself down the street toward the University of Wisconsin-Madison, his craving for hangover food, a cup of coffee, and a return to the world of the living intensifies. It's a pleasant summer morning, maybe a little bright and cool for someone who's got a massive headache and is still wearing the same tan cargo shorts and stained V-neck tee from the night before, which is still a little foggy in his alcohol-soaked brain. It started out with him hanging with his buds and getting their drink on. Later, it involved him stumbling down Langdon Street with a similarly inebriated, good-looking girl. Then, it ended with the two of them in a drunken sex romp at 2 a.m. The sex was nice, at least for him. Most drunken sex is quick, with a little foreplay followed by passing out cold instead of cuddling—much the theme of his recent single status.

This is not his preferred method of having sex, but since his latest heart-wrenching breakup, it's the most he has to offer. It seems his love life occurs in cycles: he has a lasting relationship (over two months), then a breakup, then goes through a series of one-nighters and quick-to-sex first dates until he's ready to put his heart on the chopping block again. He's on his second meaningless tryst in the past week, and it's just as unfulfilling as the previous one.

Great. Not only does his mouth taste like ass from all the beer, but now he's feeling the tug of emotional guilt over having sex with someone he barely knows. Someone he definitely does not want to see again or be in a relationship with.

As the sidewalk curves toward Memorial Union, Dek can smell the Sunday brunch being served at the campus cafeteria. He hefts open the front doors and continues to the counter for his saving grace in a foam cup. The girl behind the counter gives him a disapproving look, but he can't tell if it's the aren't-you-too-old-to-still-be-in-college look or the aren't-you-too-old-to-be-this-hungover look. Honestly, he can hardly even make her out through the blur of his bloodshot eyes. He never changed out his contacts, which are not designed for overnight wear, and they have turned his eyes into throbbing orbs of fuzzy vision. Either way, she's probably right, though twenty-six isn't too old to be a student—which he is not—and is a very common age for a teacher assistant and aspiring researcher. As for the hungover-slash-still-wearing-last-night's-clothes-slash-walk-of-shame-for-coffee, maybe she's got a point.

Regardless, he pays for his coffee and a blueberry bagel with cream cheese and proceeds through the Union to the Terrace. The staff is still setting up the orange and yellow, brightly colored chairs, the signature of the Terrace which looks out over Lake Mendota. Dek finds a private table where he can overlook the crystal-blue lake. The morning sun reflects on the tiny waves, giving off flashes of diamond brilliance.

He is two bites through the first half of his bagel and already almost done with his coffee when he hears a familiar booming voice behind him say, "I thought this is where I would find you. Did you forget something this morning? Like meeting me for our morning run and workout?"

That would be the voice of James Stratman, Dek's best friend and workout partner. He was with Dek at the start of last night's festivities but bailed out at 11 p.m. with his perfect girlfriend—and soon-to-be fiancée—Pam. He's a six-foot-five former Wisconsin wide receiver. He was a good player but didn't have the hands to make a strong enough impression at the NFL combines, so he didn't get drafted. When Dek was a senior, he was James's science tutor, and they became good friends as he helped James squeak through chemistry. James is still an intimidating specimen at 225 pounds of muscle and less than 5 percent body fat, always raring to go work out.

"Look, man," James starts, taking a seat in the chair across from Dek, "before you can even start to come up with some lame excuse, I forgive you. I saw that you had your game face on last night. You looked like a man on a mission." He leans back, stretching his arms out before folding his hands behind his head with a shit-eating grin. "So did you get laid, or were you too wasted to get it up?" he wisecracked.

"Getting it up has never been a problem for me," Dek says. "No matter how much I drink, the little general still comes out, ready for action."

"Was it the brunette in that back booth or the shorter girl you were scoping out by the bar?" James asks. "You know that I have to live vicariously through you now that I'm off the market," he adds, referring to his near-married state of whipped-ness.

"Well, my friend," Dek starts, sounding way smugger than he felt, "it was neither. Do you remember those two volleyball chicks that Sam used to talk about? He was always claiming they were so hot."

"Oh, yeah, one was blond and one brunette, both about six feet tall and hot as hell. I don't recall those two ever leaving each other's side. Please, do not tell me that you had them both. My poor taken heart couldn't stand it." He then places a hand on his chin in a thoughtful pose. "Although, that would be quite a story and ménage à trois."

Dek shakes his head and says, "Sam, Porter, and I were shooting darts at that board at the top of the stairs when the two girls walked up. Sam started in with the blond, Jill—you know he's always had a thing for blonds. That left me, the happy-to-be-of-service wingman, to tend to the brunette, Amy. Of course, Porter bails out, saying he has to get up early. Anyway, she and I stumbled to her apartment off Langdon after bar time. I think Sam took the blond back to his place."

"And ... did the little general wear his helmet?" James asks with raised eyebrows.

"Of course, man," Dek replies with a laugh. "You can't fuck around with that shit these days."

"Do you have any recollection of the actual event, or were you too drunk to remember?" James asks. "I'm begging for details here."

"She had legs forever and an awesome athletic body," Dek says, refraining from giving out any more details. He already feels guilty enough for sneaking out the door this morning before she even woke up.

"So could this one possibly be a replacement for Kelly?" James asks eagerly. He's been waiting for Dek to have a steady girlfriend again so they can double-date.

For the past two years, Dek has been in and out of small relationships, usually lasting only a week or less. Before this stint of small trysts, Dek was in a three-year relationship with a girl named Kelly. She was leggy and blond, with striking blue eyes. She had a beautiful smile and was always ready to share it. They met in one of his biochemistry classes. She was in pharmacy school, and they quickly became inseparable. They would study together and even have all their meals together. Kelly had basically moved in with him and his roommates, sharing his room. They had gone so far into the marriage side of a relationship, the fun side of dating and going out had all but gone away. James always used to call them the "little old married couple."

Sadly, Kelly graduated two years ago and got a job in Milwaukee for a pharmacy chain. She and Dek tried to keep the relationship going long-distance for a month or two, but they quickly grew apart. Then Dek found out Kelly was cheating on him with her coworker after he found some explicit texts on her phone and thus began his downward spiral. Feeling he had missed out on so much of his college experience due to his pseudo-marriage state, Dek turned into a partying machine. Even after graduating the next year, he got a job at the college as a grad student adviser and assistant to the science department to stay at school. James fears Dek will not be able to move on with his life until he gets over his reluctance to be in another serious relationship.

"Sorry, man," Dek states. "There's only one prefect Pam out there, and I think you got her. Besides, after I slinked out of Amy's apartment this morning, I'm not sure if she will ever talk to me again."

"You're a dog, Dek," James says with a shake of his head. "Anyway, I figured that you wouldn't be up for hitting the gym this morning, so I lifted at the SERF and grabbed a veggie smoothie before coming over this way."

About six months ago, James changed over to an all-vegetable diet. Something he saw in a nutritional documentary turned him on to the idea. He feels the reduction in animal products from his diet has increased his circulation, given him greater muscle stamina, and turned him into the crazy physical specimen he is today.

"Yeah, man, I feel like shit, and I have to do some work over at the lab today," Dek says, rubbing his face between his hands, trying to shake off the hangover. "I'll have to catch up Monday."

"All right, cool. I'm going to cruise. Pam and I are going to go for a bike ride around the lake later today. It looks like it's going to be a nice day," James says as he gets up. "I'll give you a call later about our workout schedule."

***

Dek stops at his rent house to clean himself up a little before walking to the lab. After a quick shower, he pauses to look in the bathroom mirror. His bloodshot, blue-green eyes stare back at him with a disapproving glare. As his father likes to say, "The main person you are accountable to for your actions is the man in the mirror. Don't be a disappointment to him." A rough night of drinking has him feeling way older than he should at twenty-six.

You just can't keep doing this, Dek.

He applies some hair gel and tussles his brown hair into a disheveled, I-don't-care-what-I-look-like style. He brushes his teeth and does a quick shave before leaving, heading to the lab to finish the carbon dating samples for Dr. Stinson's archaeology class. The lab is in an older building—probably built in the 1970s—just a short three-block walk away. It's five stories high, and there are green strands of ivy creeping up its brown brick exterior. It houses most of the university's laboratory facilities for the science department.

Walking into the lobby, Dek is taken aback when his "hot chick" radar, as he calls it, is set off by a girl arguing at the front counter with Janet, the usual lab attendant. He can't see the girl's face, but she has beautiful, sandy-blond hair and a fit body. He takes a mental note and plans to look for her later when he's not so busy.

He waves his hand at Janet to get her attention. She nods and smiles, buzzing him inside, probably making the other girl even more annoyed. He takes the stairs on the right and bounds up toward the second floor where his meager office and lab space are located. Sundays can be kind of hit-or-miss as to how crowded the lab will get. So far, he hasn't seen a soul.

The lab is separated from two tiny offices by a glass window. He unlocks his office and gets his samples off the desk. He peers into the lab and sees Richard Lancaster III, the current occupant of the other tiny office with whom he has to share the lab space. The lab is adequate workspace for two, but there is only one laminar flow hood. The hood is a tall cabinet with an open, flat work surface. If there are any dangerous gases given off by the materials, the hood will suck them up and filter them before they can become harmful. Richard is working on some samples of his own in the very hood Dek needs to use.

Dek pokes his head into the lab. "Hey, Dick, are you about done with the hood? I need it ASAP," he says smartly.

"Screw you, Dek!" Richard replies, pausing his work to flip Dek the bird. "I was here first, and I'm just getting started. Besides, my name is *Richard*! Now I'm going to take extra-long, just to annoy you. Asshole."

Richard is like *that* guy in high school who was the super-smart, trust-fund kid everyone hated because he would constantly brag about how smart he was and how much money he had. He's about five-six with black hair and even blacker eyes. He's mastered the art of the scowl, which he always wears. That is, unless he's telling someone how much better he is than them at everything, then he wears an annoying, smug grin. He also hates being called "Dick," so, naturally, Dek calls him that every chance he gets.

"Aw, come on, Richard," Dek pleads. "I have to get this work done for Dr. Stinson, or I could be suspended from the lab for two weeks."

"Not my problem. Maybe if you weren't such an ass, I would help you," Richard spits back. "I heard Dr. Martin is out of her office this week. Maybe you can figure out a way to use her equipment."

Richard knows Dek used to date Dr. Martin's assistant Jan, and he suspects Jan gave Dek a key to Dr. Martin's lab so they could fool around during lab breaks.

It happens that Richard is correct. Using the other lab is risky because if Dek gets caught, he could get kicked out of the lab for good. But today is an emergency, so he grabs his keys and samples and leaves the room.

"I'll just wait until you're done, Dick," he says. "I'll be in the library until you're finished."

Before Richard can respond, Dek zips back to the stairs and runs to the fourth floor. He peeks into the hallway ... all clear. At the lab door, his key luckily still works. The lab is a little different than he remembers it; Dr. Martin must have gotten some new equipment. The room is full of cubed lab areas, and a large hood is on the outer wall between two shaded windows.

He pauses at a mirrored medicine cabinet on the right-hand wall, looking for ibuprofen—his head is still not right. He finds some and takes two tablets. He also notices some tampons in the cabinet, which is strange since Dr. Martin is over sixty years old. Probably best not to think too hard on that one.

Leaving the cabinet ajar, Dek proceeds to the hood. Assuming Richard is going to try to get him into trouble for using a private lab and having a key without permission, he gets to work fast. There's a good chance Richard knew about the fling Dek had with Jan last year, and he could be setting Dek up to be caught using someone else's lab. Richard would love for Dek to be kicked out, giving him sole use of their current shared space.

The work Dek's doing shouldn't take long and is relatively inert. Ignoring proper hood technique, he quickly wipes down the middle of the workspace and places his samples in the center. The hood is excessively dirty for a new piece of equipment, which is odd considering Dr. Martin never allows her workspaces to have so much dust and sample fragments left behind. With a shrug, Dek just shoves all the mess to the right side of the hood and makes a mental note to do a proper cleanup when he's done.

As he sets up his samples, he notices this new hood has been equipped with a safety gate that would slam shut if toxic fumes or radiation were not being properly filtered out. He also sees the red filter light is on, indicating it needs to be changed. But the samples he's working with shouldn't release any fumes or toxins, so he commences his work, trying to rush. His samples are said to be from Machu Picchu but are most likely fakes.

He's halfway through taking a scraping from his first sample when he feels a gust of air from the door opening. Assuming it's Richard coming to yell at him, Dek ignores it and tries to finish. Suddenly, the shades pop open to the right of him, sending a ray of sunlight across the right side of the hood surface, and a girl storms in, yelling, "What do you think you're doing? This lab is highly restricted! You need to get out now!"

The commotion startles Dek, causing him to jump and bang his head on the hood. Leaning one elbow on the edge of the hood and rubbing the back of his head, he glances up to see the beautiful girl from the lobby. She's even better looking from the front, with raging brown eyes. She is still yelling at him to get out, saying this area is very dangerous.

"Okay, okay," he mutters as he bends down to pick up his samples.

The light from the outside window is shining in his eyes and face, reflecting off the partially open medicine cabinet, and temporarily blinding him. The light also reveals some of the dust he pushed to the side of the hood. A slight puff of steam starts to rise, and Dek gets a big whiff of it.

The frustrated girl moves up right next to him, thrusts the samples into his hand, and clutches his wrist, trying to pull him away from the hood. As Dek stands up, he starts feeling lightheaded. He exhales a deep breath right in the girl's face stammering, "W-what's happening?" He places his free hand on the edge of the hood to steady himself.

Then there's a huge *crash* as the hood's emergency safety door slams down on his hand. Blood explodes across his face and the girl as he slumps to the ground, the world around him going dark. The girl steps back, startled, as the spray of blood has splattered across her shirt. She momentarily braces herself on the side of the hood before passing out, crumpling to the floor.

The last thing Dek hears is the alarm sounding and someone yelling, "Dek, you dumb shit, what have you done?"

CHAPTER 2

Waking up in the hospital is always one of the worst experiences, especially if you're not sure why you're there, and this time does not disappoint. Dek's mouth is as dry as the Sahara; he can barely peel his tongue from the roof of his mouth. He can smell the distinct odor of hospital cleanser even before he opens his eyes. The room is low-lit, and it takes a minute for his eyes to adjust to the spectral glare of the lights. It's a basic square room with what looks like a bathroom in the right-hand corner. He notices there are no windows. He must be in the ICU or some kind of trauma center. As he tries to sit up some, he realizes he's restrained. His heart starts to race, and he anxiously looks about, trying to figure out what's going on.

James is sitting in a chair next to the bed, watching *SportsCenter*. He jumps up when he realizes Dek is awake. "Hey, man, just chill out," James stutters, seeing Dek struggle.

"I'm tied up. Why? What's going on?" Dek exclaims.

"Wait, wait, wait," James says, holding out his hands in a calming fashion. "They tied you down so you don't hurt your hand anymore by accident."

"Jesus!" Dek yells, looking down at the mound of bandages covering his hand. He can't believe it, but his hand is freakishly swollen. "What the hell happened?"

"Aw, man, you don't remember? It got smashed by the safety mechanism of the hood you were using." James sighs sympathetically.

It all starts to come back to Dek in a blur. "Did I lose any digits?" he asks hesitantly without looking up.

"Yeah, man, a couple of them," James replies.

Dek almost starts to tear up as the gravity of the situation smacks him in the face. *A couple of digits ... how am I supposed to type, to play sports, to live?* He thinks in a rush of panic.

James must've realized Dek was about to spiral because he quickly tries to bring him back to Earth. "It's okay, man, lots of people have lost a lot more than that and can fully function in their lives. Think of some of the veterans that we play hoops with at the gym. Some of those guys are in way worse shape than you."

"Oh, yeah ... shit, man, just give me a minute. I just woke up, and you dump this on me," Dek says, trying to shake the cobwebs out. "God, why did I pass out in the first place?"

James rests his hand gently on Dek's shoulder. "My friend, that's what I and a whole lot of other people want to know. Why were you in that lab anyway?"

Dek leans back in the bed. "Oh, shit, I think I really fucked up this time," he says, talking more to himself than James. "I was in a time crunch, and Dick was in our lab using the hood. I remembered that I still had a key to Dr. Martin's lab and went up there to get my samples done. Am I out of a job?" he asks, shaking his head in disgust.

"I'm not sure," James says with a sigh. "The dean called yesterday to check on you. He didn't sound too happy. Lab injuries are a big deal if you're in your own lab, let alone messing around in someone else's."

"'Yesterday'? How long have I been in here?" Dek blurts out.

James hesitates for a moment before saying, "It's been two days. You got hurt on Sunday, and it's Tuesday now."

"For a *hand injury*? That doesn't make any sense."

"I think that whatever chemicals you took in must have knocked you for a loop," James says. "And being so hungover probably didn't help the situation."

"What could it have been?" Dek asks in disbelief. "I've had plenty of rough nights before, and nothing like that has ever happened."

James's eyes light up a little like he just figured out a joke. "Hey, you know what? I talked with Janet at the front desk when I went back for your things. She said that a girl who was using Dr. Martin's lab was doing all sorts of crazy upgrades. Ordering new equipment and using special radiation filters for the hood. Maybe, if she was doing something sketchy, you could prove it and get off the hook with the dean."

The thought is definitely encouraging. The girl he's talking about must've been the one Dek saw arguing with Janet when he walked in that morning, the one who came up to the lab and surprised him. All he remembers about her face were those amazing, raging brown eyes.

As if on cue, the door to his hospital room slams open, and two women come pushing in. One of them is a nurse trying to hold back the very girl the guys were just talking about. "But miss," the nurse argues, "he's not conscious. You can't just barge in here! I'm calling security."

"I need to talk to him!" the girl insists. "He owes me some answers!"

They both pause as they notice Dek is, in fact, awake.

Then the nurse immediately runs to his bedside. Looking at James, she angrily asks, "Why didn't you call me? I could've gotten the doctor right away. His condition could've been fatal!"

During their one-sided conversation, Dek keeps his eyes on the girl at the door. She's looking at him with an angry but sad look, as though she feels guilty for what happened to his hand. *She's so beautiful*, he thinks. That, he did remember correctly.

Then the rage starts to come back in those unforgettable eyes.

When the nurse is done lecturing a frightened James, she rudely pushes past the girl and exits the room. "I am still getting security and the doctor!" she yells from the hall.

The girl wastes little time scolding Dek. "What do you think you were doing breaking into my lab? And what crazy chemicals were you experimenting with? Clearly not approved samples! What did you do to me?" Her tone changes at the end of her rant, as though she's pleading with him to give her an explanation. Then the doctor and a hospital security guard burst into the room.

"This young lady is not authorized to be here," the nurse states, entering just after the security guard.

"Come on, miss, you have to leave," the guard states, grabbing her arm to drag her out of the room.

As they leave, she looks Dek right in the eye and again asks, "What did you do to me?" before disappearing around the corner.

Dek turns to James, absolutely stunned.

James gives him a half-smile and asks, "You knocked her up, didn't you?"

Oh, good grief!

Before he can gather another thought, the doctor asks James to wait outside, already shining a light in Dek's eyes.

After about an hour of poking and prodding, the doctors give Dek a break. He guesses it's after visiting hours because they say James will have to come back tomorrow to take him home.

Dek is exhausted after such a short time of activity and tries to sleep, but his mind is racing. *Who was that girl, and what did I do to her?* he thinks. *I've never met her before in my life. What was she doing with radioactive samples in the lab? What will my discipline be from the school? Will I keep my job? Not to mention, how will I deal with my new life as a person with a disability? I'm absolutely terrified of seeing my mangled hand. It's probably super gross!* These are just a few of his thoughts as he drifts off to sleep, aided by painkillers and emotional exhaustion.

***

The nurses come in at least three more times throughout the night. Dek thinks it's to make sure he's still alive. At 6 a.m., the doctors come around again to change his bandage and check on his progress, and Dek gets his first look at what used to be his left hand. His pinky and ring fingers are completely gone. He's lucky to have a hand at all. Most of the remaining bones and tendons are either torn or shattered. The pain is intense as the doctors clean and redress the wound.

When they're finished, they tell Dek he needs to stay at the hospital for at least twenty-four hours after he wakes up, and he should be able to go home tonight. It's kind of a relief, but he still can't wrap his mind around what his life will be like going forward. He contacts James and asks if he can pick him up around 8 p.m. once James finishes tutoring a fellow football player at 6:30.

It's dark out when Dek finally exits the hospital. It's quiet, and he feels like a weight has been lifted from just getting out of there. *I hate hospitals.* The ride is short as James drops Dek off at his house. It's an old, two-story house tucked behind Lupe's Garden, which is famous for its seven-foot-tall sunflowers. There's a long gravel driveway, and the house is at the end, almost hidden behind a three-story apartment building.

He waves goodbye to James, then walks up the front porch and enters a musty-smelling front room. Dek rents the house with two roommates who aren't there since it's summertime, so he has the whole place to himself for a while. There are two bedrooms upstairs on either side of the stairway. The one on the left is his. There's one more bedroom downstairs, along with a bathroom and a little kitchen with old but functional appliances. The backdoor connected to the kitchen is used for storing bikes. They don't have an air conditioner, so Dek uses his right hand to open some windows and let in the cool night air.

He goes to the bathroom to take a piss, then looks at himself in the mirror. His skin looks pale and drawn with dark circles under his eyes. "I look like shit," he says to his reflection. He goes to the kitchen to throw a frozen pizza in the oven and pops open a cold beer before sitting down on the couch to watch some TV.

Once he's got a full stomach, he takes some painkillers and heads up to bed. Even when propped up on a pillow, his hand still throbs. He stares up at the darkened ceiling. It's been a long time since he's had any significant injury. The last he can remember was breaking his leg during football practice in his senior year of high school. His younger brother, only a sophomore at the time, was on the team with him, and their dad was an assistant coach. Dek can still remember the looks of concern on the caring faces of his teammates and family as he was helped off the field. His leg healed quickly, but the injury forced him to realize he would never be a pro football player and allowed him to refocus his life on science.

Hopefully, I didn't just fuck all that up, he thinks as he falls asleep.

***

That night, Dek has some crazy dreams, probably due to the meds. He keeps dreaming he's in an Etch A Sketch. In the dream, he's inside the toy and slowly moving with the smooth, aluminum powder, perfectly in control, forming a straight line. Then suddenly, he feels himself being jerked all over the screen, making a scribbled, indecipherable mess, as if someone is cranking the dials back and forth as fast as they can. Dek wakes up in a sweat, his heart racing, making it almost impossible to breathe. *God, my life is spiraling out of control*, he thinks as he stares up at the dark ceiling.

The next morning, he falls out of bed at 10 a.m. Luckily, he drew all the blinds in the house before he went to sleep, because his eyes feel very light-sensitive right now, and he can tell the sun is shining brightly outside through the cracks. He eases his way downstairs and grabs a diet cola from the fridge. He walks out on the porch, shirtless and in shorts, shielding his face from the sunlight with his good hand. "Well, I can't just sit around and feel sorry for myself," he says to himself, taking in a confident breath. He's about to walk down the porch steps when he feels dizzy and falls down the stairs. He lies there on the gravel driveway in the sun, his body bleeding from the crash and shielded from the street by the neighbor's car.

CHAPTER 3

A group of businessmen are conducting a meeting in a long boardroom. A wall of windows flanks a large, very expensive wooden table lined by five leather chairs. Each chair is filled with a suit listening to a presentation involving spreadsheets and graphs.

At the head of the table is a large man in a gray suit. He is about sixty years old with salt-and-pepper black hair. He has a round, stern face with a bulbous nose and is clearly the boss. When the cell phone near his hand starts to buzz and vibrate, he nods to the man on his right named Miles Feldman who takes the phone and exits to an adjoining office.

Feldman, the reigning vice president at Helms Chemical, discretely positions his tall, reed-like frame behind a desk in the side office before answering the phone. "Feldman."

"Give me the big guy," a voice on the line demands.

"He's in a meeting," Feldman says dryly. "Is there a problem?"

"We had an incident at the lab. He said to let him know if anything happened near his precious samples."

"What kind of incident? You need to be very clear about everything that happened."

"Yeah, okay. Someone snuck into the lab and was using the hood. Something triggered the safety mechanism on it, and it slammed shut, cutting off part of the guy's hand. Because we removed some of the fail-safes to cover what we were testing in the hood, the normal safety stops failed."

"Are the police involved?"

"No, not that I know of. But the university is starting an investigation."

"How did this person gain access to our project area?"

"He had a key to the lab from Dr. Martin. The key was obtained prior to our setup. We didn't change the locks, not wanting to draw attention to the project."

"The testing was complete, and the test materials were already sent off," Feldman confirms, agitation showing in his voice. "Was the area cleaned of all evidence of what we were doing except for the hood?"

"I wasn't the one doing the cleanup, and Dr. Summers was also involved in the accident."

"Was Summers hurt?"

"No, she's okay. I guess she surprised the guy and passed out. Maybe from some fumes or shock or something."

"You have been removed from the project, effective immediately. I will handle it from here on out. Distance yourself," Feldman orders before abruptly ending the call. He then hits the contacts icon on the phone's screen, scrolls down to a number marked "V," then presses the call button.

After one ring, a voice picks up on the other end. "Vincent."

"I think we have a problem in Madison. Are you almost done in South America?"

"I've been working with the police to find out what happened to the drilling crew. It seems that the guide we had was working with some Colombian gangs and led them to a clearing over the border to set up their rig. They were ambushed, and all were killed. The guide was killed as well. We recovered some of the equipment, but it's in bad shape. The Ecuadorian government is working with the Colombians to see if they can figure out who attacked the drilling crew. I have talked with our contact to set up the drilling rights to the sites we identified in Ecuador. We should be good to go in a few months. He's working on fast-tracking our way through the government's red tape. What happened in Madison?"

"The samples were tested and sent off. Someone broke into the lab and was injured on the special hood that we developed for the tests. I am afraid it will bring unwanted attention to what we were doing there. I need you to go and clean up the area. I want the hood and anything to do with the tests gone."

"I'll take care of it. I can be there in twenty-four hours."

Both men hang up, and Feldman returns to the boardroom, making brief eye contact with the boss man seated at the head of the table as he sits down.

CHAPTER 4

"Oh my god! Don't be dead. Please, don't be dead!" Dek hears a muffled voice yell into his ear. His head is pounding as he feels himself being lifted and carried up porch steps into a house. He can hear the creaking of the wood beneath their weight and the sound of a door being opened.

"Are you okay? Are you all right?" says the same voice, shaking him gently after setting him down on a couch.

Dek slowly opens his eyes and waits a moment as they start to focus on the person looming over him. *It's the girl from the lab ... here in my house.* He looks around to find the guy who carried him inside to thank him, but it's just the two of them. Surely, this girl didn't carry him on her own.

Then he sees the half-eaten pizza on the table and beer bottles strewn about the floor and feels slightly embarrassed. *Man, I'm a pig.* "What happened?" he asks, snapping back to the situation, though still a little groggy.

"You tell me," she states, backing up a bit. "I just found you lying on the ground outside on the driveway. There was blood on the ground and on your skin, but you don't appear to be hurt."

Dek quickly looks down at his hands and arms. There are spots and smears of dried blood but no injuries, not even a skinned elbow. He gets up with the girl's help and walks to the bathroom to wash up and check the rest of his body. She's right, he looks scary. He has dried blood crusted in his hair and on his face and neck. He still doesn't see any wounds though.

There's a small knock, and he sees the girl leaning against the doorframe. "Are you going to be all right?" she asks, still looking a little concerned.

"I don't know," he quietly admits, then begins to clean himself off with a warm washcloth, looking for a large gash or at least a scratch. Instead, he realizes he looks better than ever.

The girl comes in to help him due to his injured hand. "You must have been lying out there for most of the day," she says, wiping off his back. "You look like you've got a good sunburn on most of your back."

In a few minutes, Dek's clean and discovers that, surprisingly, there are no signs of him having been hurt. He and the girl are both silent, not quite sure what to make of it. They walk back to the living room and sit on the couch.

"Were you in a fight?" she finally asks, cautiously. "Did you get attacked?"

He slowly shakes his head, trying to remember what happened. "I just went outside, stretched, and then everything went black."

He looks at the girl as he talks and finds he's very attracted to her. He can't stop staring into her eyes. He was right about how amazing they looked. Now that he's calmly looking at them, he can see they aren't just brown but have a lighter hue, like a starburst around each pupil. She has a small, round face perfectly framed by her full, flowing hair. There's a slight curl to her hair, accentuated by blond highlights ending just below her shoulders. He must've leaned toward her unconsciously because she pulls her head back about an inch and smiles, a hint of a blush on her pale cheeks.

He gets the sense he's been caught and quickly straightens back up, shaking his head. "So, anyway, who are you? And why do you keep showing up in my life?"

She straightens up too, probably realizing she never properly introduced herself. "My name is Lauren Summers. I was doing some contract work in the lab before *someone* broke into my private space and destroyed my life," she says, giving him a look. "Who are *you?*"

The girl has definitely got an attitude. "I'm Decklan Thomas, but you can call me 'Dek.' I work in a lab two floors down. My hood was being used, and I was in a time crunch. I knew Dr. Martin's previous assistant and I had a key to her lab. I didn't think anyone was using it so ... Anyway, how did I 'ruin your life'?" he asks, mimicking her sarcastic tone.

"I already knew your name," Lauren says. "Remember? I saw you at the hospital. I guess what I really want to know is what you were working on and why we both had such an extreme reaction to it."

"I have no idea. It makes no sense to me. I was just doing some carbon dating on some probably fake relics for Dr. Stinson. I don't think there was anything crazy about my samples. What were *you* doing? Rumor has it that you were doing some sketchy stuff, like working with radiation that required major safety equipment to be installed ... or uninstalled. I noticed that the safety closure that removed part of my hand had the safety stops deactivated."

"I get the feeling you think this is some kind of tit-for-tat situation, but it ends here. My project is not open to the public. I took every precaution and followed all the safety protocols with any radioactive samples that I may or may not have been working with. My employers are very serious about their privacy. Did *you* follow any rules at all while doing your tests?"

Lauren has him there. Dek bypassed proper and safe handling procedures, but his samples were nothing. How could they have caused the accident?

"Look," he says, feeling a little defensive. "My stuff was still there, and I'm sure you looked it over. What do you think? Yours or mine?"

Even when she looks totally pissed off, Dek can't stop thinking about how beautiful Lauren is. *What's wrong with me? This is serious, and all I want to do is kiss those plump lips.*

Again, she seems to be reading his mind, giving a knowing look and blushing slightly. "You need to mind your own business … and stop leering at me," she scolds.

He feigns being appalled by the implication, but based on that sexy raised eyebrow, she's clearly not buying it. He clears his throat and decides it's time to change the subject. "So what did you mean when you said that I did something to you?"

She seems to have been waiting for this question. She takes a slight breath before lighting into him. "Whether it's due to your negligence, laziness, or stupidity, you have risked my career, my reputation, and my life in that 'accident,' as you call it. The people that have contracted me are serious, and I think there's a large sum of money on the line. They value my being discreet, and you just ruined any chance of that."

Before he can defend himself or even mount an apology, she adds quietly, "And ever since the accident, something's been wrong with me. I think that what happened to you today is similar to what I've been experiencing."

When she doesn't elaborate, he asks, "What do you mean?"

"After we collapsed, the paramedics came in and were able to revive me, but you remained unconscious. I was taken to the hospital and treated for some minor scrapes and bruises. When I got a ride to my apartment from a police officer, I felt okay, but the sun was really bothering me, hurting my eyes and giving me a headache. All the same, after about ten minutes in my room, I felt the need to go outside, to get some fresh air. I went out to a bench on the side of my apartment building, and basically, I passed out on it. I woke up a little after seven. I'd been on the bench for *four hours*. I somehow pulled myself up and went back inside, but I don't remember much about being on the bench except the warm and comforting feeling of the heat on my skin. I should've been seriously sunburned, but I only saw a slight sign of one. In fact, my injuries from the accident were completely healed. No marks or scratches. I actually looked better than ever. I rarely pamper myself, and I've been under so much stress lately, it would take a jackhammer to remove the circles under my eyes from not sleeping at night." She pauses a moment to finally take a breath. "Anyway, I chalked it up to needing some fresh air and sat down to watch TV. My eyes couldn't focus, so I thought there must be something wrong with my contacts. I took them out and put on my glasses, but I still had the same problem. When I removed my glasses to clean them, I realized that my vision was perfect without the glasses, even though I've needed them since the fifth grade!"

There's silence as Dek lets everything she just word-vomited sink in. "Okay, wait ... you're saying that something we encountered at the lab is healing us?" he asks.

"Yes!" she shouts, sounding both nervous and excited.

He must've been giving her a look because she angrily says, "Look, I'm not crazy. I've had bad knees since junior high. Now, they feel great! Plus, I'm, like, crazy strong. I lifted you on my shoulder when I brought you in the house earlier, and you're a grown man!" She stands up and walks around the room, talking quickly and gesturing animatedly. "I can't fully explain it, but all my senses are running at an acute level. I can hear, smell, taste, and feel things that I never could dream of before. I can smell the old beer cans in the sink in there," she says, motioning to the kitchen. Honestly, Dek wishes she *couldn't* smell them. God knows how long they've been sitting there. "I can hear the hum of your alarm clock upstairs and the TV in your neighbor's apartment."

She's trying to prove a point, but Dek is still unsure. "That's not exactly amazing, you know," he says with a hint of skepticism. "It could just be because you finally got some much-needed rest."

Lauren throws her arms up, obviously frustrated. "Oh, come on! You fell outside and were significantly injured, if that pool of blood drying on your driveway is anything to go by, and now you're healed to the point that there's not even a scratch on you. Look, I know it sounds insane or superhero-like or whatever, but I *know* I'm not the same today as I was three days ago. Something's changed, and I think it's because of whatever we were exposed to in the lab."

"Okay, I'll admit that some strange things have been happening since the accident, but right now, my hand is destroyed and hurts like hell, so can you help me change the bandage really quickly?" Dek asks, holding up his injured hand.

"All right," Lauren says with a sigh, sitting down on the couch next to him. She helps him unwrap the gauze and remove some of the blood-stained pads. She cringes, closing one eye and cocking her head to the right as they remove the last concealing pad.

Then they both freeze.

The stitches used to close the wound have come undone and fallen out, and the two fingers that were cut off have mostly grown back! The skin is soft and red, like a newborn's.

Dek looks up at Lauren, her eyes are wide, and he can tell from the smug grin on her face that she's dying to say, "I told you so." She holds off, though, taking his damaged hand in her own and palpitating the wound and the new fingers. "You said that it hurts. Does it hurt when I touch it?" she asks.

Dek shakes his head. "No, I think maybe it was hurting because the wrap was not put on with the idea that we may need room for new fingers to grow." Even as he says it, he still can't believe it. *For fuck's sake, chopped-off body parts don't just grow back!* "This can't be possible," he mutters to himself as he sits there, looking at his hand. He was so worried before about living the rest of his life with a deformed hand, praying that time would rewind so he could do it all over and have his fingers back. Now they're growing back right before his eyes, and he's got a cocktail of emotions swirling in his stomach—scared, relieved, nervous, excited.

Lost in thought, Dek nearly jumps out of his skin when he hears someone trying to open the locked front door. "Knock, knock! Hey, Dek, you in there, man?" It's James.

Dek looks at Lauren, then at his hand. She quickly shakes her head and covers his still slightly wounded hand with her smaller, softer one. She leans in to whisper in his ear, and he can smell a hint of coconut shampoo in her hair. "Not till we know what's going on." Then she gets up to unlock the door, leaving Dek on the couch, trying to calm himself down.

James saunters inside. "Hey, man, since when do you lock—" He stops mid-sentence when he notices it was Lauren who opened the door. "Oh, um, hi … I thought you two didn't know each other."

"James, this is Lauren," Dek says, gesturing her way. "I just met her a few minutes ago. It seems we both had a reaction to something at the lab, and she came by to see if we could figure it out."

"Yeah, you know, since we both passed out," she adds quickly, giving him a look that says not to go too far with his explanation.

"Well, I was just coming by on my way to the gym to check if Dek needed anything, but I can see you're in good hands, dude," James says as he starts to inch closer to the door, looking sheepish, as if he thinks he just intruded on an intimate moment. That's when Dek remembers he's still shirtless. "By the way, I think the cat next door must have gotten hold of a squirrel or something. There's blood on the ground by the steps."

"Oh, I did hear something this morning," Dek blurts out at the same time Lauren quickly says, "I did see something while walking up."

Yeah, Dek thinks, *talking nervously over each other isn't suspicious at all.*

James gives him a knowing look, clearly thinking they were fooling around before James arrived, then says, "Mm-hmm … anyway, I'll catch you later, man. Let me know if you need anything. Nice meeting you, Lauren." Gently closing the door, he heads off down the driveway.

"We should have told him," Dek says, feeling guilty for keeping his best friend in the dark. "He's a good guy and really smart. He might even be able to help us figure this out."

"That may be, but right now, I just have the feeling the fewer people who know about this, the better," Lauren says, returning to the couch and picking up his hand to look at it again. "Let's keep this wrapped up for now. What should be our next move?" she asks, gently applying a new, clean bandage to his healing hand.

Once she's finished, Dek slumps back on the couch, feeling a little exhausted from the whole his-crazy-hand-injury-is-healing thing. "Well, this all started in the lab. I think that's the most logical place for us to look and figure out what may have happened. Although, I no longer have access to anything and won't until the dean decides what to do with me, so I won't be any help getting in. Not to mention, they'll be shutting down the lab for the night soon," he says, looking out the window at the setting sun.

"I have a key to the building and the lab," Lauren states, excited she may have a partner to help her figure all this out. "It's at my apartment. You up for checking it out now?"

"Cool," Dek says, getting up from the couch, then gives her a sideways glance. "Wait, how do you have a key to the building?"

"I told you; I was doing a very important project for people with a lot of money. Now get dressed and let's go," she says, heading outside to start her car, and clearly hiding something.

CHAPTER 5

Lauren drives them to her apartment complex just down the street from the stadium called Langdon Place. It's a seven-story building usually for upperclassmen or grad students, not at all the party area of campus. She parks in a lot about a block away, and the two of them walk to the front entrance.

As they walk through the lobby, Dek is shocked to hear a familiar voice say, "Dek, what are you doing here? I thought you were badly hurt or something." He turns and sees Dick quickly walking his way, no doubt excited to rub the lab incident in his face.

"Hey ... Richard," Dek says, not really feeling up to calling him "Dick" just to piss him off as he normally does.

Richard stops short when he notices Lauren. "Who's your friend?"

"This is Lauren," Dek says. "Lauren, this is Richard. He shares a lab with me."

Richard eagerly shakes Lauren's hand. "Hi, beautiful. You better watch out for this guy. He's a bit of a menace." He then turns his attention back to Dek, glancing down at his bandaged hand, and asks, "So what happened to you the other day?"

Dek fights back the urge to roll his eyes. "I had a little accident with some safety equipment on the hood in Dr. Martin's lab," he says, waiting for the next snide remark.

"Dek never was much of one for protocol," Richard comments, looking at Lauren and laughing nervously. "I heard you lost your hand."

"Great exaggeration. Should be good as new shortly," Dek says, wincing when Lauren elbows him in the arm and gives him a shut-up-you-idiot look.

"Well, Richard, it was nice meeting you, but Dek and I are kind of in a hurry," Lauren says, taking Dek's good hand and leading him toward the elevator.

"Oh, yeah? What are you guys up to?" Richard asks nosily, following them.

"I don't know, maybe watching a movie," Dek says as they wait for the elevator.

"Oh, sounds like fun! Hey, I'm going up too," Richard says, trying to continue the conversation. "So you live here too?" he asks Lauren. "I haven't seen you here before."

"Yes, I moved in a few weeks ago," Lauren says a bit coldly, keeping things brief.

The elevator opens, and they all get in. "What floor?" Richard asks, manning the buttons and remaining very cheery.

"Five," Lauren replies.

Dick pushes the buttons and turns back to talking her up. "So are you a student here? Dek and I are grad research students," he states.

"I'm doing some independent research," Lauren says. She stares up at the elevator numbers, trying to indicate she doesn't want to chitchat.

The doors open, and they exit, relieved to escape the awkwardness of the small space. "Hey, this is my floor too," Richard says, smiling. "Room 503."

"Bye, Richard," Dek and Lauren say as they wave to him without looking back and continue walking down the hall to Room 513.

After they get in and close the door, Dek says, "You live on the same floor as Dick? I feel for you."

"Yeah," Lauren says with a sigh. "He's been giving me weird looks since I moved in, and he totally knows that I'm working in the same lab building. I've seen him there at least half a dozen times. He always gives me the creeps." Her disgust is emphasized by a little shoulder shiver.

"Okay," Decklan says, sitting on a soft pleather couch. "What's the plan? It's after hours, and I'm definitely not allowed back in the lab without talking to the dean first."

"Would you like a drink?" Lauren asks, as if she didn't even hear him. She calmly walks into the kitchen, trying to portray the exact opposite of what she's actually feeling. Whatever's going on inside their bodies is scary and exciting at the same time. She glances back at him, waiting for a reply. She doesn't even know this man sitting on her couch, but he seems to be genuine. She's surprised by how safe she feels when she's alone with him. Maybe it's the changes, but she feels like she's known him for a long time.

"Sure," Dek says, leaning back, like they have all the time in the world. "Got any beer?"

He tries to relax, not sure where she's going with this, and takes a minute to look around her little apartment. It's very clean, at least, by his standards, which honestly aren't very high. It looks like she's staying in a hotel room rather than living here, which makes him wonder how long she intends to be in Madison. *Is she just passing through for work? Using our lab for her project, then moving on to the next big thing?* He'd do that himself if he had the guts to get out there.

Lauren hands him a beer and sits next to him on the couch, holding a glass of water.

"Making me drink alone? I see how it is," he says, offering up his glass for a cheers.

She clinks glasses with him and says, "You know, I was thinking about going it alone to the lab for the very reasons you stated earlier." Before he can protest, she adds, "You can come with me as a getaway driver or lookout of sorts." She takes a drink, raising her eyebrows hopefully.

"I think we both need to be in there to figure this out. Two eyes are better than one," Dek says. "Really, I need to know what happened in there. This is too big to just leave it with what you found out."

Lauren grows quiet, trying to read him again. "So you feel you need to go to get some closure or something?" she asks, giving him an understanding nod.

Dek lets out a small laugh. "I'm not sure if all my thoughts are written on my face or what, but that's pretty much what I had in mind. You're scary good at knowing what I'm thinking," he says before throwing his beer back and standing up. "Let's go."

"Hold on a second," she says, motioning for him to sit back down. "Let me check on your hand and talk over what we're even looking for."

As he returns to the couch, Lauren takes his injured hand and starts to gently remove the bandages. Dek's heart starts racing and feeling her skin on his causes his mind to wander again. His lust for her is beginning to scare him. He's not usually this horny, not even around a beautiful woman. So what makes Lauren so special?

When his hand is completely unwrapped, it seems to look very similar to the last time they looked at it. There's maybe a slight amount of additional growth. "Seems to have slowed down," Dek says, feeling a little defeated having hoped for greater progress.

"That's what I was expecting," Lauren replies, piquing his interest. "I think that whatever has occurred has some correlation with oxygen or fresh air. All of our experiences, or, at least, our strongest reactions, so far have happened when we were outside."

Dek is trying to pay attention, but the way she's caressing his injured hand is making it hard. "I think I see where you're going. Me passing out on the steps and you on the bench could be due to fresh air or a pollutant in the air that we're now more sensitive to," he says, pulling his hand back slowly, causing her to give him a confused look. "Sorry, I just can't concentrate with you touching me. It's kind of turning me on," he says with a shrug. *Might as well be honest.*

Lauren blushes and looks away sheepishly. "I was testing you a little with that too," she replies.

"Testing me by flirting with me?" Dek asks. Then it dawns on him. "That's not what you meant, is it?"

She shakes her head. "My hormones have been acting on overload since the accident. I think that, along with my senses getting stronger, my natural ability to give off and receive hormonal and pheromonal responses is heightened. I feel strongly attracted to you and wanted to test if I was invoking the same response."

"You most definitely are," he says, lowering his voice and leaning in. "Do you want to act on any of those feelings?"

She rolls her eyes and pushes him back. "If I were to act on them, I would need to have far more knowledge of what caused them first. I think that it's important to understand our condition. It may be something we can use to our advantage."

Dek relaxes back into the couch, trying to look nonchalant despite his hurt pride. He's not used to being rejected. "Are you sure? With this kind of a spark, it could be *epic*."

She just gives him an exasperated look. "Clearly, it's having a major effect on you and your ability to think things through. We should use our sexual enticements to influence people to let us in the lab, even if they might not want to."

"You think it will work?" he asks, a little stung by his advances getting shot down so easily. "I didn't have much luck coaxing you into bed just now."

"I doubt the desk clerk will be dropping her pants, but she may be more inclined to look the other way. Besides, I've already tried it, and it worked very well," Lauren says with a grin.

Dek instantly sits up and gives her a fake how-could-you look. "What? You've had this 'power' for only three days and are already using it for your own gain?"

Lauren lets out a small laugh. "How do you think I found you at the hospital and was able to get into your room? Of course, I was too frazzled when I got in there to try it on the nurse to stop her from getting security."

"You really are a mystery, Miss Summers," Dek says, slightly in awe. *Beauty and brains ... a woman after my own heart.* "Shall we go and try to flirt our way into the lab?"

"Let's," she says as she heads toward the door, grabbing her keys from where she tossed them earlier. She pauses for a moment before turning to him and adding, "You know, you may be underestimating the effect you're having on me. We'll have to take a rain check on finding out for now." Then she throws him a quick wink and walks out the door, Dek following closely behind her, barely able to hide the large smile on his face.

CHAPTER 6

They exit the apartment and decide to approach the lab on foot. It's only about a ten-minute walk and a beautiful summer night. On the way, Lauren tells Dek more about the hood she was using, still leaving out what exactly she was working on. They decide they need to get to the lab and check the test area once they get into the building. Then they'll try to find the hood filter to see if some particles were trapped during the test and not properly cleaned up after the accident. The usual procedure after a lab accident is to have the scene fully cleaned and sterilized to prevent any further exposure, but the cleanup crew may have missed the filter.

They walk casually past the front glass doors to peek in and see who's on guard duty. "All right, this is all me," Lauren says, turning toward Dek as they clear the doors. "That's Ed in there tonight. I don't think I'm going to have any problem with this, so you go around to the side door, and I'll let you in."

Dek crouches down and scurries over to the side of the building near the loading area to wait.

Lauren runs her fingers through her hair, then taps on the glass doors. Ed, a thirty-five-year-old heavyset guard, walks up to the glass and shines his flashlight on her. She gives a little wave and says, "Hey, Ed, I need to get a few things from the lab."

The guard opens the door, "Evening, Dr. Summers. They're still working to clean up that accident and investigate what might've gone wrong. I'm not sure I can let you up there, especially after hours," he says, keeping the door open just a crack.

"I understand, but they took me out of here in the ambulance, and I wasn't able to get some personal items out of the lab. Can you please make an exception, just this once?" Lauren pleads as she leans in a little closer, pushing her breasts out and trying to release just enough pheromones to make Ed more complacent.

Blushing and looking toward the ground, Ed swallows hard and says, "I guess it's okay. Want me to take you up there?"

"No, no, I wouldn't want to get you in any trouble. I'm just going to take some things to my car out the side door. I'll just be a few minutes," Lauren says, easing her way past Ed.

"Let me know if you need any help with anything," Ed says as she quickly walks down the hall.

"Thanks, Ed, you're the best!" Lauren replies before disappearing around the corner toward the side door. "Okay, let's hurry," she whispers as Dek makes his way inside. "I got the impression Ed thought I might be in the mood for a little lab sex or something. He may come looking for me if we take too long."

"Lab sex, huh? Sounds explosive," Decklan adds with a smirk, causing her to give him a look that could kill.

"Focus!" she hisses and turns toward the stairs.

When they reach the top of the stairs, they peek out into the hallway to make sure the coast is clear. It's dark in the labs, but the emergency lights at the end of the hall are on, the soft-yellow tint giving an unwelcoming glow. They get to the lab door and find it's unlocked. They give each other a concerned look before going in.

"Would someone leave this unlocked if they were investigating?" Dek asks. "It seems strange, not to mention dangerous."

Lauren doesn't answer, just goes to her desk and turns on the desk lamp to give herself enough light to look through her desk without bringing unwanted attention. She then pulls out a small flashlight and walks toward the hulking hood at the back of the lab.

"What are we looking for?" Dek asks, still dying to know the details of her secret project.

Lauren stops in front of the hood. "Damn, the filter has been removed!" She stands back to survey the scene of the accident. "You were here at the hood, bending over to look at some samples," she says, pointing to the front-left side of the hood.

"I was just cleaning them off to begin," Dek says. "I don't think I really got started before you came in."

Lauren walks over to the right side of the hood. "I came in here and opened the shades," she says, making the motion with her hand. "I was facing you." She walks toward the hood. "I was mad that you were in my space and going through my personal things."

"'Going through your personal things'?" Dek echoes. "You're kidding, right? I was just using the hood, not snooping around in your stuff."

Lauren turns around and motions toward the mirrored medicine cabinet on the wall. "I noticed when I came in that someone went through the cabinet. What, were you looking for a tampon?" she asks sarcastically.

Dek scoffs. "I was hungover and looking for some ibuprofen," he says, feeling attacked. "How did you even know I looked in there?"

"The cabinet was still hanging open when I walked in. Anyway, I walked toward the hood and asked you what you were doing," she says, walking back toward Dek to continue her reenactment. "Then you stand up and suddenly fall into me, steadying yourself on the edge of the hood, then the gate smashes your hand." She straightens up. "What am I missing?" she asks, looking over the path she just walked.

"I was in a hurry to get this done and get out, so I didn't properly clean the area, just kind of pushed the dust on the hood off to the side. What were you working with? Could that have given off some kind of radiation or chemical?" Dek asks, trying to get at the nature of her testing, certain it holds the answers they're seeking.

"I already told you I have a confidentiality agreement," Lauren says, a little annoyed. "I was testing some radioactive substances, but the samples were already mailed off, and I had thoroughly tested the area and checked the hood for any signs of radiation. All that was on the hood was some dust that I had cleaned off the samples. Nonradioactive! I then went down to the front desk to get some more cleaning supplies to finish up. When I came back, an *interloper* had snuck into my workspace." She crosses her arms and raises an eyebrow at him.

"Let's think about this," Dek says, running his hand through his hair in frustration. Then he catches a bit of movement out of the corner of his eye. Grabbing Lauren's hand, he pulls both of them closer to the floor. "I think Ed might've come up to get some action," he whispers.

They both peek over the counter and see a man standing in the doorway, looking directly at them. "I don't believe anyone is allowed in this room. It's under investigation," he says firmly.

Dek and Lauren slowly stand up with their hands out in front of them in a calming motion. Then Dek relaxes when he notices the man's rubber gloves and trash bags, realizing this guy is probably a janitor, not a cop. "Hey, man," he says, "I'm a grad student. I was working in this lab before the accident. I just came to see if I left any of my stuff here."

"And I'm the lead researcher in this lab," Lauren breaks in, trying to intimidate him with her status. "We're trying to determine what caused the accident."

"Why are you guys doing this in the middle of the night and not during the day?" he asks, with a strong New Jersey accent. "You guys could be in big trouble. The investigators and cleanup crew who were here earlier are very serious about their jobs."

Wanting to get the guy to trust them so he doesn't call security, Dek decides to make an introduction. "My name is Decklan, and this lovely lady is Lauren. We were involved in the accident and are just trying to figure out what happened. We're not trying to get anyone in trouble here."

Noticing Dek's bandaged hand, the janitor man seems to relax a little. "Okay, my name's Vince, and I've been working here for just a few days. I'm not sure what you're looking for, but I think you'd better leave."

"We just need a couple of minutes, and we'll be done," Lauren says quickly. "Do you know who removed the filter from this hood?" she asks, pointing to an empty slot at the side of the hood near the air vent.

Vince walks closer to the hood to look. "Nope," he says simply. "I would guess one of the cleanup crew."

Lauren opens the lower cabinet on the hood and reaches up and to the left. She pulls out a smaller filter about the size of an envelope. "At least they didn't get this one," she says triumphantly. She places it in a plastic bag she retrieved from one of the desk drawers.

"Maybe you should let me have that," Vince suggests, trying to get a better look at the filter. "The police and cleanup crew will probably need to see it."

Suddenly, there are loud footsteps pounding down the hallway. Dek and Lauren once again duck down behind one of the tables, and Vince follows suit a few rows away. The lab door bursts open, and Richard comes in panting. "Dek, Dek, are you in here?" he gasps, trying to catch his breath. He must've run all the way up here.

Dek groans and stands up, along with Lauren and Vince. *Unbelievable.* "Dick, what the hell are you doing here?"

"Look, no time," Richard stammers, still trying to recover from running up the stairs. Probably the most he's worked out in years. "I saw you guys leaving the apartment, heading this way, and figured that you might be returning to the scene of the crime, so I followed you."

"First off, we didn't commit any crime. Second, where do you get off following us here?" Dek growls.

"Dek, we have to go!" Richard says, trying not to crumble under their angry, piercing stares. "I think Ed saw me sneak in the back and called the cops!"

Lauren and Decklan run to the window and see two police cars pulling up in front of the building.

"Shit, Dick, what did you do? We're going to be arrested!" Dek exclaims, turning toward the door.

"Look, you kids, I know a way out through the basement. You can use it to avoid the cops," Vince says, motioning them to follow him out into the hall.

Richard finally notices the three of them aren't alone. "Who's that guy?" he asks, gesturing toward Vince.

"He's the night janitor and may be our savior," Lauren says, darting around the lab tables for the door, still gripping the bag with the filter. "Now let's get the hell out of here!"

They all exit the lab and dash for the stairs with Richard bringing up the rear. The others can hear his pathetic panting as they race down the dark staircase. They pass the first-floor door and head down another level toward the basement. They freeze when they hear the police officers enter the stairwell just seconds after Richard rounds the corner.

Dek holds his good hand over Richard's mouth to stop his heavy breathing. "Settle down," he whispers as the sound of the policeman's footsteps echo up the stairs toward the floor they just left.

"This way," Vince whispers, continuing down into the basement. It's pitch black, so they follow Vince's flashlight to a door near the side of the building. "This is the rear fire exit," he says, opening the door to another pitch-dark area and directing the group with the light. "It's about twenty feet to a stairway out."

Richard and Dek go first, followed by Lauren. "Hey!" she yells as she crashes into the boys, causing them all to fall into the room.

The door slams shut, and any light from the flashlight vanishes.

"What are you doing, Lauren?" Dek hisses in the dark.

"That asshole tried to grab the filter from me, then pushed me into you and slammed the door closed!"

"Who, Vince?" Dek asks. "He must think that having the filter will help him keep his job."

"I'm not so sure ..." Lauren says, feeling her way back to the door and pushing against it. "It's locked!"

"Okay, stay calm," Richard says. "We just need to find our way across the room to the exit."

"I didn't see an Exit sign," Dek says. "And you know what? I think we may be on the wrong side of the building. Let me try to get my bearings."

Lauren lets out a small shriek when glass shatters on the ground.

"I think you're right," says Richard. "I just knocked into a beaker."

Realization dawns on Dek, who now feels like a colossal idiot. "Shit! Guys, I think we're locked in the basement storage room."

CHAPTER 7

Without any light in the room, it's dark as hell. They can't even find their balance, never mind a way out of this mess. Dek hears another crash to his left and figures Richard just knocked over a test tube or beaker again. He then feels Lauren's soft hand take his and pull him close. A very welcome feeling, he must say. Her smell is intoxicating, which isn't super appropriate, given their current situation, but it helps him calm down some.

"Dek," she breathes in his ear. "Remember what we talked about? Me not needing glasses and hearing better?"

"Yeah ...?" he whispers back, not sure where she's going with this.

"Well, I've been concentrating on it, and I can see in the dark too," she says.

"That's just your eyes getting used to the dark, Lauren," he says, not wanting things to get any worse by someone panicking.

"No, I'm serious. Try it for yourself," she urges.

He sighs but starts to concentrate on trying to see. After a second, he can actually feel a change in his eyes, and the room starts to lighten in his field of vision. It feels kind of like when the eye doctor flips the lenses, asking if one or two is better, one being pitch dark and two lighting up the whole room. It's like he's wearing night vision goggles. *This must be similar to a nocturnal animal's sight.* He turns and looks at Lauren, amazed by how beautiful she is in any light.

She cocks her head a little to the right and gives him a little smile. "Now you believe me?" she asks knowingly.

They're interrupted by the sound of more glass breaking. Now that he can see clearly in the darkness, Dek sees it's another beaker.

"My eyes aren't adjusting at all!" screams Richard, keeping his arms pinned tight to his chest to avoid breaking anything else.

"It's okay, Richard," Dek says, taking Richard's arm and leading him to a safer spot. "I can see pretty well. Must be all those late nights out, drinking in dark bars. Improved my night vision." He notices Lauren is examining the door, probably looking for a way out. He starts to look around for something he can use to force open the door.

"I think it's real wood," Lauren reports, knocking on the door. "Very sturdy."

Dek finds a broom and flat-bladed shovel in a back corner. The cleanup crew must use them so they don't cut their hands on broken glass. "Let me try this," he says, slamming the blade of the shovel into the doorjamb. He pushes with all his might, but it doesn't budge.

"Let me help," says Lauren, moving in next to him and pushing on the shovel's handle.

Crack!

The shovel breaks, and they fall against the door with a yelp.

Dek stands back up with a groan. "We don't have time for this crap! That janitor could be back any minute with the police to turn us in." Feeling pissed and needing to let off some steam, he lowers his shoulder and sidekicks the door. Shockingly, it busts wide open. "Holy shit ... I've never kicked anything that hard before in my life."

Not wasting any time, Lauren grabs his arm and pulls him out of the storage closet and into the basement. "Nice one, Dek! Let's go. Hurry!"

"Wait, this way," says Richard. The poor bastard has been through a lot tonight, so Dek figures he may as well start calling him by his real name. "That guy was half-right. There *is* a lower exit, he just took us to the wrong side."

They run across the space and find a hallway marked with a red Exit sign. They plow through the door at the end, assuming it may trigger an alarm or, at least, alert security to an open door. Glancing around quickly to make sure they're in the clear, Dek finds that even the few streetlights make his night-vision-adjusted eyes hurt. They then run across the street toward a strip mall and round the corner, out of sight from the lab's windows.

"Wait," whispers Lauren. "Walk slow and clumsy, like you're a little drunk. The cops will think that we're just walking home from the bars."

"Yeah, good idea," Dek says with a nod.

Slowing to a stumbling walk, they continue for about three blocks in silence toward Lauren and Richard's apartment complex.

Finally, out of sight, Lauren says, "Okay, seriously. What *was* that back there?"

"I can't figure it out," Dek says. "The janitor seemed to be helping us, then he locked us in that room. I assumed he was going to get the police to turn us in, but if that's true, why didn't he just let them catch us in the stairwell?"

"I don't think he was a janitor," says Lauren. "He tried to take the filter from me as he pushed us into the storage room, so maybe that's what he was after. But why?"

"Maybe Dek was onto something earlier. He was probably just trying not to lose his job for allowing us to take it from an accident scene," Richard chimes in with a shrug.

"Either way, they know our names, so I'm not sure it's safe to go home," Dek says.

"I think it's safe for *me* to go home. No one has accused me of having anything to do with the accident," says Richard excitedly. "I can help you guys. I'll go back and get some supplies and my car, and then I can pick you guys up."

Dek ponders on that for a moment, then, turning to Lauren, says, "He's got a point. I mean, he's pretty much involved now." She just gives a small shrug, so he takes that as an okay. "All right, Richard, we'll go and get some food and a beer at the Varsity. We'll meet you in about an hour in the parking structure right behind it. Sound good?"

"Yeah, Dek, sounds great. I'll meet you in an hour."

"By the way, thanks for helping us out back there, man," Dek adds.

"No problem," Richard says, walking briskly off toward the apartment. "See you in a bit!"

***

Walking to the Varsity would normally take about fifteen minutes, but Dek and Lauren decide to follow along the railroad tracks and take the back way to State Street, hoping to avoid the major streets and anyone who may be looking for them. The tracks are quiet and smell strongly of tar.

After a moment, Dek takes Lauren's hand, telling her it will make them look more like a couple and less like fugitives, but he really just wants the comfort of holding her hand. They walk in relative silence for several minutes, still trying to process the night's events.

Eventually, Lauren asks, "Do you really trust Dick ... um, Richard?"

"I don't know," Dek answers honestly, timing his steps to only walk on the beams. "He seems to want to help."

"He gives me the creeps though. I keep getting the feeling that he isn't being honest," she says as they leave the tracks and walk up to the bar.

The Varsity is a typical college bar. The smell of burgers and fried food coming from the back kitchen masks some of the spilled beer and cheap cologne stench in the main bar area. The lights are dimmed, making the primary source of light the many TVs scattered behind the bar and on the walls, playing the current sporting events of the season. There's a long bar lining the left side of the room, and small tables and booths along the right side. A bank of windows behind the booths looks out onto State Street, making it a great location for people-watching.

Dek and Lauren go in and grab a back booth with a good view of the sidewalk and front door. Dek orders some food and goes to use the restroom. When he gets back, Lauren says she's running over to the ATM machine to get some cash. He watches her from their booth, and from the way it was just spitting out money, it looks as though she's retrieving a large sum.

"How much money did you just get?" he asks as she returns to the booth. "It looked like you just won the fucking lottery from the way it was dumping out cash."

"I got out a couple thousand," she says calmly, like that was a perfectly normal thing to do. "If I just messed up my confidentiality agreement with my employer, they may try to take back their money, and I want to have some in hand so they can't take it all. Besides, we may need some cash if this thing gets as crazy as I think it could."

"You may be right," Dek says, sweating a little over the fact that he barely has a few hundred dollars in his account. He *knew* he should've worked for the private sector instead of the university. "Well, we have another miracle," he adds, trying to keep things light. "Night vision? I mean, c'mon!"

"I'm not sure what changed us or how it works, but I agree. It's very cool," she says with a smile, glancing over as the waitress brings their food. They eat like ravenous dogs, devouring their hamburgers and fries in minutes.

Taking a breather from his meal, Dek asks, "Do you think it's, like, some kind of superhero accident in the lab that gave us superpowers? I'm not gonna lie, I can't wait to see what happens next."

"The only problem is that we don't know if this will kill us or make us that much better. We also seem to have acquired some villains along the way. That was crazy back at the lab," Lauren rationalizes, taking a bite of her french fries. "What if there are people after us?"

The thought makes Dek glance cautiously around the bar, though nothing appears to be out of the ordinary. It's the same thing anyone would find in a college bar any day of the week. A couple of dudes are playing darts, and small pockets of friends are chatting over beer. Dek finds that if he concentrates, his hearing improves to the point where he can pick up random conversations here and there throughout the bar. The girls at the bar's end think the guy who just walked by is *sooo* cute. Someone in a side booth is stressing about a bad grade he made in his summer chemistry class.

Lauren puts her hand on Dek's forearm. "Don't worry. That guy really wasn't all that cute," she says, smiling at him.

"You were doing it too?" he asks, giving her an incredulous look.

"I can't believe how well I can pick out detailed conversations all over the bar. There are two girls in a booth over by the front door, saying how one of them picked up a guy at a bar the other night and had a totally unfulfilling one-night stand. She was overjoyed that the guy had left the next morning while she pretended to sleep, not even wanting to talk to him."

He shakes his head and finishes off his beer. "We have to figure this out. Where do we go from here?"

Lauren pulls back and thinks for a minute. "Let's get out of town. I have some friends in Chicago who may be able to help us," she says before signaling the waitress for the check. "I got it," she adds, pulling enough money from her wad for their meal and tip.

They pay the tab and walk toward the front exit. As they head near the door, one of the girls sitting in a nearby booth gets up to go to the bathroom. Dek pauses as he recognizes the girl he went home with the night before the accident. "Hey, Amy," he says awkwardly, giving her a slight wave.

"Hey, Dek," she replies, giving her friend a *that's him* look before continuing to the bathroom.

Lauren suspiciously looks back at Dek as they walk out onto State Street. The smells coming from the college bars lining the road are almost overwhelming. Beer, puke, piss, perfume, and greasy food … what a great place to live.

CHAPTER 8

In the meantime, Richard walks into his apartment building and hurries to the elevator. He nervously pushes the 'up' arrow and shifts his weight from side to side as he waits for the doors to open. He nearly runs over the people trying to exit as he darts in and pushes the button for his floor and the one to close the door at almost the same time. After what feels like an eternity, the doors open on his floor, and he rushes down the hall to his apartment. His nerves make his hands shake, causing him to have trouble getting his key in the lock. All the while, he's looking over his shoulder to make sure no one was watching him.

Finally, he gets inside and slams the door shut, locking it and leaning his back against it as he takes a deep breath. "What the hell have I gotten myself into?" he asks aloud.

Pushing off the door, he starts pacing and talking loudly and quickly to himself. "All right, all right, all right. Why does Dek always seem to make colossal mistakes that affect my life too?" he complains, waving his arms demonstratively. "*He's* the screw-up but still ends up with the girl. Why do I have to go out of my way to help him not get in even more trouble? Because Lauren wants to keep the testing she was doing under wraps? She shouldn't have overseen doing those tests in the first place! It should've been *me*, then none of this would've happened. Now I have to drive these two lovebirds around like their damn chauffeur. And what the hell was that janitor doing, locking us in the lab storage room? I can't believe the night I've had. If it wasn't for me, we never would've gotten out of there."

"That's good to know," says a deep voice.

Richard spins around, looking for where the voice came from. "Who's there? I've got a gun!" he lies, trying to find something to defend himself with.

The janitor from the lab—*What's his name? Vince?* —emerges from Richard's darkened bedroom. "I know you don't have a gun, Richard," he says menacingly. "I'm not sure you would know how to use one if you did."

"What are you doing here? How did you get in?" Richard exclaims, his voice raising an octave with each word.

"I work for the same people who hired you to keep an eye on Miss Summers and not let their project get exposed to any unnecessary attention. You have obviously failed, and, therefore, I was sent here. You can call me Mr. Vincent," the not-really-a-janitor says, entering the room. He pulls out a dining chair and faces it toward Richard. Sitting down calmly and crossing his legs, he asks, "Why don't you fill me in on what's going on so far?"

"You're not the boss of me," Richard says, trying to regain some control. "I have high-up connections. High-up! So, don't try to intimidate me. What happened at the lab was a crazy accident. I had *nothing* to do with it." His voice cracks a little as the man shifts in his chair, still staring Richard right in the eyes. "It was that idiot Dek."

"Decklan Thomas just decided to use the lab to test some samples of his own. The samples gave off a gas, chemical, or radiation that knocked out him and Dr. Summers, who surprised him during his test. The substance triggered the safety protocol on the modified hood, and it crushed Decklan's hand. Is that what happened as you know it, Richard?" Mr. Vincent calmly confirms.

"Yeah, I guess that's right. How do you know so much about it?"

"I have my sources. The question that I have is why are the two young doctors together, searching the lab for filters and evidence of what was being tested in the hood?"

"Dek's not a doctor. He's a teacher's assistant and not a very good one at that," Richard says snidely. "I don't know why they were together. I didn't think they even knew each other."

"Mr. Thomas has earned enough credits for multiple doctorates if he put them together in one field. How did you end up following them to the lab tonight?"

"I saw them together here in the lobby. I knew they were up to something, so I followed them to the lab. I thought it was better to not have them caught by the police in the lab."

"That was wise, but I wanted to question them in the basement after the police left. How did they get out?" Mr. Vincent asked, continuing his interrogation.

"I'm not really sure. I couldn't see a thing. I think Dek kicked the door or something," Richard replied, naïvely feeling a little more comfortable with the conversation.

"I had hoped to find them back here. Do you know what they're planning to do?"

"Yes, I'm going to drive them out of town. I already had a plan of my own to keep tabs on them," says Richard smugly, believing he has more knowledge than the big bad Mr. Vincent in this matter.

"Very good, Richard. I will give you my cell number, and you will text me with your location and any information you can get from them. I feel that this little babysitting project has gone badly so far, but I will judge your usefulness over the next days' time," Mr. Vincent says coldly, sending a shiver down Richard's spine.

"Uh, okay," he says, nervous again. "What if they ask me who I'm texting?"

"A smart guy like you will figure it out," Mr. Vincent replies. "Give me your phone. You had better get ready. I assume you will be leaving soon."

Mr. Vincent puts his number into Richard's phone and activates an app that will allow him to track the phone's location.

In the meantime, Richard runs into the bedroom and starts getting some things together, cursing under his breath. "Who does this guy think he is, bossing me around?" Coming out five minutes later with a duffel bag stuffed with clothes and supplies, he rudely says, "Can I have my phone back? I'll be leaving now. Will you be getting out of my apartment, which, by the way, I never invited you into in the first place?"

"Richard, I'm on your side here," coos Mr. Vincent. "Act normal and let them tell you where they want to go. Do as they ask and text me with the information. I put the number in your phone under 'V.'" Mr. Vincent stands to exit the apartment, adding, "Don't do anything stupid. I'll see you soon."

"'On my side,' my ass," Richard says under his breath, locking the apartment as they leave and allowing time for Mr. Vincent to enter the staircase before going to the elevator. "I never should have accepted my stepfather's offer. Every influence he's ever had in my life has been negative."

Richard's biological father was a drunk and often erupted into anger at the slightest misstep Richard or his mother made. Worst of all, things always seemed to go his father's way despite his issues. He would get fired from one job only to walk right into a better one. Richard hated how easily everything fell into place for his shitty father. He was truly relieved when his father finally split and divorced his mother.

Afterward, Richard and his mother lived quietly together for a few years until she met Mr. Helms. Richard's mother was a bank teller, and Helms would continually come in, making big deposits and flirting with her. He was ten years older than her and not at all good looking. Richard believes she only agreed to date and eventually marry Helms because he's rich. She'd always wanted Richard to have more opportunities and a better life, and she probably thought Helms's money could provide all those things.

Looking back, they would've been better off without Helms. Things were good for the first few years of their marriage, but after a while, Richard began to feel like an outsider. Helms never paid much attention to him and made it very clear he should be thankful to be the stepson of a rich and powerful businessman who could give him all the things he wouldn't have otherwise.

By the time he was eighteen, Richard was sick of feeling indebted to Helms and longed to be out from under the shadow Helms always seemed to cast over him. He was happy to go away for college and did well, hoping he would soon be able to leave and go out on his own. He just needed some more capital, then he could get his own lab started. That was when an opportunity came up through the beloved Mr. Helms. All Richard had to do was find a lab, get everything set up, and watch Lauren Summers work from afar to make sure nothing crazy happened, and he would get fifty thousand dollars in the form of a graduation gift to get himself started. It would've been easy if he hadn't lost his cool with Dek, sending him straight to the restricted lab area to fuck everything up.

Dek has always reminded Richard of his biological father. He cares little for being responsible and is always out drinking and womanizing while Richard studies or works in the lab. They always seem to be neck and neck in the eyes of the professors who oversee their work, no matter how much better and smarter Richard clearly is. It has to be this jealousy that pushed him to make that error the morning of the accident, but he's not going to let that happen again. He refuses to let this chance to be out on his own and away from his stepfather slip away. He'll do what Mr. Vincent told him and let the chips fall where they may for Decklan Thomas.

**

A few minutes later, Dek and Lauren see Richard's car pull into the parking garage behind the Varsity. He drives up and says to them with a rather cheery nervousness, "Your chariot awaits."

Dek and Lauren exchange glances as they get into the car. "We'll ride in the back in case someone is looking for us," Dek says, pushing the front seat forward for Lauren to climb into the backseat. "We were thinking of going down to Beloit and finding a hotel off the highway to get some shuteye. What do you think, Richard?"

"You're the boss, Dek," replies Richard, again seeming a little nervous.

Maybe it's just the running-from-the-law thing that's making him act weird, Dek thinks.

A sudden bang on the driver's side window causes all of them to jump.

A man dressed in old, ragged clothes appears and asks, "Hey, man, can you spare some change?"

Startled and annoyed Richard yells, "Take a hike!"

The man then peers into the back of the car at Lauren who decides to roll down her window and hands him five dollars.

"Please, just spend it on food," she says as he eagerly grabs the money.

"Thank you and God bless," says the man, backing away from the car, still staring at them.

As they pull out, Richard scoffs. "He stunk of alcohol. You know he's going right to the liquor store with that money."

"I hope not," Lauren says, yawning.

Dek puts an arm around her, and she snuggles into his chest. "Is this okay?" he asks quietly. She gives only a slight nod of her head in response. It's been a long night, and they both need a little rest and comfort. After such a stressful day, Lauren is emotionally and physically drained. She's not sure what it is about Dek, but she finds herself feeling more attracted to him and thinking the little things he does are endearing. Like the way he was kind to their server at the Varsity, or even just the way he shifts his head when she says something that surprises him. She was a little concerned at the way he got nervous after seeing the girl at the front of the bar, with whom he clearly had some kind of relationship. Two days ago, she was ready to kill him, and now she feels comfortable and safe in his arms. She smiles softly and closes her eyes, letting the hum of the car soothe her to sleep.

As they drive out of Madison, Dek spots the lit-up capital building towering high on a hill, marking the center of town and the start of State Street. He can't help thinking this is probably just the start of a long journey.

CHAPTER 9

Dek wakes up the next morning with a feeling of exhilaration. They spent the night at a Best Western, and Dek squints a little as the sun peeks through the hotel's curtain, shining on his face. He looks over at Lauren, sleeping quietly on the queen-sized bed beside his, and finds it strange to be waking up next to a girl he didn't just have sex with. To top it off, he doesn't even want to run out the door before she wakes up.

It's been a while since he's let himself get so close to a girl without being intimate. His latest run of single dates or one-night stands has made him more skeptical of finding real love. Lately, he's been conflicted. One the one hand, he wants to find love again, but on the other hand, he's afraid of being hurt again, so he decides within ten minutes into a date that she's not the one he's looking for and ends things quickly. Most times, when he hasn't had a lot to drink and is thinking clearly, he prefers going to bed alone rather than feel the sting of guilt that comes the morning after a night of meaningless sex.

Dek finds it hard to pull his eyes away from Lauren's serene face, but he's afraid it'll freak her out if she wakes up and catches him staring at her, so he eases out of bed. He realizes his hand is still bandaged since they didn't want Richard to find out about their strange powers, so he decides to go outside and take a look at it, feeling the need to have the sun on his skin and curious to see if his hand has healed any more since yesterday. He grabs a room key and quietly exits their first-floor room and walks down the hallway that leads to the parking lot.

He feels an instant shock of resurgence as the rising sun caresses his bare chest and face. This time, he doesn't pass out. Instead, he widens his arms and embraces the welcome heat. He's yet to have any coffee but feels like he needs to go for a run or do some kind of exercise. It's been almost a week since he last worked out. James would say he's losing his edge.

Wearing just his shorts and tennis shoes, Dek starts to run along the side road next to the highway. Sometimes, he only feels like jogging a little when he runs, especially after having a rough night, but this morning, he's sprinting like an athlete in training. His energy level is unfailing as he runs at full speed down the road. His legs seem to be responding to his every need, pushing him faster and stronger with little to no sign of fatigue. When he glances down, it looks like the ground is flying by, like when he looks out a car window. He finally decides to stop and turn back when he realizes he's a good ten miles from the hotel. He's been running with James for years but never for this long at that pace, and he feels great. He's not tired in the least.

He takes a deep breath and starts running back. This time, he concentrates on the run. Legs pumping, he's going faster than he ever has before at almost a full sprint. For a moment, he's lost in the euphoria, just feeling the warm sun on his back and his muscles working perfectly without any fatigue. He's back at the hotel twenty-five minutes later. That's about two to three minutes per mile, faster than any Olympic athlete. He's winded but feels like he could keep going. He shakes his head and tries to do some cool-down stretches. He glances up as he hears clapping to catch Lauren hopping off Richard's car bumper and walking toward Dek.

"Bravo!" she says, slowing her clap to a stop. "You looked great out there. Ready to give Usain Bolt a run for his money." She's always thought Dek was a handsome guy from the moment she met him, but seeing him run without his shirt on definitely sent her heart into overdrive.

"I can't believe it," Dek says, resting his hands on his hips as he tries to catch his breath. "I could never dream of running that fast or that long. I just ran twenty miles!" he exclaims, a big smile spreading across his face. "I feel great! Hungry as a horse but great."

"I'm feeling it too," Lauren replies, rubbing her stomach. "It must have something to do with the fresh air. It seems to be powering me up."

She looks great too, Dek thinks. With that slight just-got-up tussle to her hair, she is glowing in the sunlight.

"I would run with you, but I've had knee problems since I hurt my leg doing gymnastics as a kid," she explains.

"I really need to eat," Dek says, straightening back up. "Let's wake up Dick and look for some food. Are we going to Chicago today?"

"That's the plan," Lauren says.

Feeling exhilarated after getting outside, they quickly walk back into the hotel room to find Richard awake and doing something on his phone. He looks up nervously as they come in, like they caught him doing something wrong.

"Hey, Richard, you looking at porn so early in the morning?" Dek teases, sitting on the base of the bed.

"Not that it's any of your business, but I have things that I'm scheduled to do in my life. If I just decide to wake up and drive to Beloit, I need to let my appointments know that I won't be there," Richard whines, letting them know they should be grateful for wasting his precious time on helping them.

Dek holds his hands up in surrender. "Okay, sorry, man. I didn't realize how much of a burden we were. If you want, we can just take it from here. We'll rent a car and be out of your hair. If you leave this morning, you can be back in Madison by noon. No need to cancel appointments."

Richard gives him a hurt and worried look. "No, I can drive you guys," he quickly says, changing his tune and placing his phone in his pocket. "You don't need to rent a car. I just sent the texts, so it won't make any difference if I'm back or not for a few days. Where are we going next?"

"Really, Richard, it was so nice of you to drive us out of Madison, but we can rent a car," Lauren adds, feeling she and Dek will be able to talk more freely and figure out what's going on with them without Richard around. "I'm not sure if we're in trouble for accessing the lab last night, but we wouldn't want to get you any more involved. You go back. We'll be fine."

"Guys, I insist," Richard says firmly, now seeming desperate to stay with them. "I want to help. If I'm gone, it will seem less likely that I could've been with you at the lab last night. I sent a text this morning saying that I left yesterday and will be gone for a few days. If I go back now, I'll look like I might've been involved."

Dek and Lauren share a look, both wondering what's got Richard all wound up. He's talking in circles and not making much sense.

I guess it couldn't hurt to have him tag along a little while longer and save us the hassle of renting a car, Dek thinks. "All right," he says, grabbing a towel and shirt. "I need to take a shower real quick. Then let's get out of here and get some food. I'm fuckin' starving."

After Dek's shower, they all gather their things and check out. They decide to go across the street to Cracker Barrel for some breakfast, and Dek proceeds to pig out on at least three entrees. He even inhales anything Richard doesn't finish. The dude eats like a bird.

Once they finish and pay the check, they get in the car so Richard can drive on to Chicago. Lauren is anxious to find her friend at Northwestern University and analyze the filter they took from the lab. She and Dek don't tell Richard this friend is also a biochemist who may be able to help them figure out what's going on with their bodies.

During the drive, Dek sits in the back with Lauren as she attempts to change the bandages on his hand. To their surprise, it's healing at a much faster pace than before. The fingers are almost normal size again, and the nails are starting to reform. The stitching from the surgery has fallen off, and a slight scar is visible on the outside of the hand. He can move the fingers slightly, meaning the tendons and muscles are coming back, but he still has no feeling in the new fingers. It may take longer for the nerves to be fully restored. They give each other a shocked look, and Lauren quickly covers the hand so Richard doesn't see, as he's straining to catch a glimpse in the rearview mirror.

"Hand's pretty much a loss, huh?" Richard asks just as Lauren finishes wrapping it.

Dek sits back in his seat with a sigh. "It's actually not that bad. I think it'll be okay," he replies, giving Lauren a knowing smile. Hopefully, if he downplays the injury, it'll be easier to explain later why the hand is completely healed.

"I heard the whole outside of your hand, including some fingers, was cut off," Richard says, giving Dek a confused look in the rearview mirror.

"No, it was crushed but not cut off," Dek lies, setting more groundwork for explaining his hand, should Richard see it later. "You know how people exaggerate."

***

There's a nervous, excited energy in the car as they reach Northwestern University located on the east side of Chicago on the shore of Lake Michigan. It's a beautiful, state-of-the-art campus still brimming with life, even on a hot summer morning. Lauren directs Richard to a lab building on the southeast side of campus marked "Bioengineering."

Leaving Richard in the car on his phone again, Lauren and Dek walk in to ask the front desk attendant to call down Lauren's friend Dr. Harold Strong, her previous instructor and mentor. He's one of the foremost experts in bioengineering and genome mapping. They arrived shortly before noon since he agreed to meet them for lunch. When he arrives, Dek is surprised by Dr. Strong's appearance. He's about fifty years old but looks more like a surfer dude than a professor in his tan shorts and surfer's T-shirt. He has a tan face with white, shoulder-length hair and is wearing black, boxy glasses that he pushes back up his nose every three minutes. He stands about six feet tall with a small beer belly that hangs slightly over his belt. Despite his relaxed style, he speaks with confidence and knowledge, demanding everyone's attention.

After introductions, they all head back out to the car, where Lauren and Dek try to convince Richard to wait for them in the lobby so they can talk more candidly with Dr. Strong. In the end, they have to settle for Richard driving them and waiting across the street at the library. He seems adamant about not leaving their side, like he thinks they'll ditch him at their first chance.

During their lunch with Dr. Strong, neither Dek nor Lauren feels comfortable revealing too much information in a crowded restaurant, so they just talk about the accident and how they both passed out. They hint at experiencing some side effects that may be triggered by outside air or some external source. Dr. Strong's interest is piqued enough to invite them back to the lab later that afternoon. His last class wraps up at 3:30 p.m., so they can meet him at 4 p.m. He can then take some blood samples and see if they have some sort of blood poisoning.

Lauren pays for their meal as a thank you to Dr. Strong, then he heads back to campus for his next class, and she and Dek walk across the street and find Richard at one of the library tables, looking at a medical book on injuries, healing, and rehab.

"Anything interesting?" Dek whispers as he and Lauren take seats in the two chairs across from him.

"Not really," he says, looking up. "How 'bout you? Find out anything about the filter in your *private* meeting with Dr. Strong?" Clearly, he's upset about being left out, but they're still not sure if it's safe to let him in on what's going on just yet.

"We're going to meet him at the lab this afternoon to take a look at it," Dek replies, ignoring Richard's remark and irritated tone. "You know, man, you don't need to keep babysitting us. We really appreciate your help so far, but you can still go back. I feel bad that we can't include you in everything that we're doing."

"It's the fact that I was working for a private firm when the accident happened," Lauren explains, trying to help Dek. "I can't let too many people find out about what I was testing for confidentiality reasons."

"How do you know it was what you were testing that was the problem?" Richard questions. "Maybe it was the samples Dek was working with that caused the accident. I've heard of fake artifacts being used to import drugs. Maybe there was some fentanyl or cocaine remnants on the samples?"

"You may be right," Dek says. "But we have to talk about Lauren's confidential work in order to figure it out."

"Look, all I'm saying is that I can help you guys. I'm smart, and I know science. If you guys let me know what's going on, maybe I'll have an intelligent thought to add," Richard pleads, seeming genuine for once. Before Dek can respond, Richard's phone starts to vibrate. Glancing down at it, his face crumples into a grimace. "I have to take this," he says gravely before picking up the phone and getting up to leave the room.

"We'll go across the street for a soda," Dek says to the back of Richard's head. Shrugging at Lauren, he motions to the coffee shop across the courtyard. "Shall we?" he asks, giving her a half-bow and a sweep of his arms in a vain attempt to be charming.

As Dek and Lauren head out the door, Richard walks to a private corner of the room and answers the call on his cell. "Hello, Mr. Helms. How can I be of service today?" he answers with a smartass undertone to his voice.

"Richard, you know I said that you can call me 'Dad' if you like," answers Helms with a sigh, being equally antagonizing. "Anyway, I'm calling to see how you're doing in Chicago."

"I'm afraid you'll always be 'Mr. Helms' to me, dear stepfather," Richard replies sarcastically. "And how do you know that I'm in Chicago? Mr. Vincent must be on a tight leash if he has to report every dump I take to you."

"Mr. Vincent is very thorough and makes regular reports when projects of such a high sensitivity level are put at risk," growls

Helms, not giving Richard a chance to make another snide remark. "This was supposed to be a *simple* observation task, but it's turned into a fucking mess that I'm getting sick of hearing about. This was your chance to prove your worth to me and this company, and so far, it's been a clusterfuck! If you think in that small brain of yours that giving me any attitude in this instance is wise, boy, then I would suggest that you think again." Helms pauses to let his words sink in. "Once more, what is your progress on controlling our current situation?"

"Sorry, sir," Richard says through clenched teeth. "It won't happen again. I've just finished driving Thomas and Summers to Chicago to meet with Dr. Strong. They've set up a meeting with him this afternoon. They say that it's to discuss the filter and what may have caused the accident, but I think they're hiding something."

"I don't understand. What do they want with that filter if they're not after the materials that we had Summers testing? Are you within their confidence on what's going on? Will you be at the meeting?" Helms asks, calming down and getting to business.

"No, sir, they're keeping me at arm's length," Richard says, sensing the disappointment on the other end of the line.

"I would suggest that you get yourself into that meeting. We need to know what they're planning in order to act appropriately," Helms says with another sigh of exhaustion at having to continually tell his stepson to up his game.

"Yes, sir," Richard replies solemnly.

"If you can't handle this, Richard, then Mr. Vincent will," Helms adds menacingly. "This is *very* important. There's a lot of money on the line. Summers and Thomas will be dealt with one way or another. Do they suspect anything from their encounter with Mr. Vincent at the lab?"

"I don't think so. They were freaked out by being locked in the basement, but I told them the guy was probably trying to save his job. I think they bought it. They seem to have formed this tight bond very quickly. They don't want to let me in," Richard complains, attempting to sound more informed about the situation than he actually is.

"Do you think they knew each other prior to the accident? Could they have been working together when Thomas got hurt?" Helms asks, wondering if they intended to steal the technology he's trying to develop from the very beginning.

"No," Richard quickly replies. "It's more of a romance thing. They're constantly acting like a love-starved couple. It's sickening."

"Well, if their relationship is so young, then it may be time to plant some seeds of doubt," Helms says, sounding as though he enjoys manipulating the players of the game. "I'll have Mr. Vincent send some incriminating texts to Miss Summers. Make sure Thomas checks her phone. If we divide them, it'll be easier to discern what they know."

"Yeah, okay. I'll try," Richard dutifully replies, feeling less thrilled with his role in all this.

"Don't screw this up, boy, or it could be *your* head on the chopping block," Helms adds as he hangs up the phone.

Richard dramatically shoots the bird at the blank screen on his phone. "Asshole," he whispers under his breath. "I still don't see what Mom ever saw in you ... besides money, I guess." Then he takes a deep breath and walks across the street to the little coffee shop where Dek and Lauren are having a drink.

***

On the other end of the line, Helms sets his phone down on his desk and pinches the bridge of his nose, trying to stop his head from throbbing. "That fucking piece of shit always thinks he can talk back to me," he growls to Feldman, who's sitting patiently on the other side of the desk.

"I suspect he had a larger role in the accident than he's letting on," Feldman calmly replies. "At least he's managed to stay with them. Maybe we can get some intel that will help us decide how to proceed."

"I'm beginning to think this should be handled just like the geologists in South America—quick and permanent," Helms says, nodding to himself.

"Sir, that was in the middle of a Colombian jungle, and the scientists didn't even know where they were. This is in the middle of an American city and could become an even bigger mess if not handled properly," Feldman reminded him.

"True, but I have every confidence in Mr. Vincent. The way he handled South America was brilliant. Do you remember that? First, he took the scientists to all the sites in Ecuador where we believed the metal was located, having them draw up the samples that we truly desired but telling them the very radiation signature given off by the metal we were seeking was the one thing they were to avoid in their testing. They went around, finding all our dig sites but reporting failure. Then, when the sites were all flagged and the true samples were gathered, he took them to the last site and pretended to have not noticed that they were over the border into another country where a civil dispute was taking place. A very dangerous civil dispute which, unfortunately for them, had some unintended casualties." A smug, wicked smile creeps across Helms's face as he leans back in his chair. "Ingenious."

"It's just too bad that your stepson couldn't handle his rather simple job. Mr. Vincent says he'll proceed with candor. I'm starting to suspect that this may not end well for Summers and Thomas," Feldman adds as he gets up to leave.

***

Entering the coffee shop, Dek and Lauren are hit with the comforting aroma of espresso, brewing coffee, and freshly baked pastries. The room is cozy with about five small tables spread around a counter and a pastry display case. Finding a table with relative privacy, Lauren sits down, facing the door, and Dek goes to the counter to place an order. Lauren takes a minute to enjoy a moment of peace, looking out at the bustling street. She looks over as Dek is finishing his order and sees the college-aged barista flirtatiously smiling and giggling at some corny crack he must've made. She feels a slight twinge of jealousy while watching the interaction and turns her attention back to the door before he notices her watching him. It's crazy, but she kind of feels like she wants to be the one fake-laughing at his less-than-funny jokes.

"The smell of this place was driving me crazy from across the street," Dek says, putting a tray with two coffees and a plate of pastries on the table. He grabs a seat next to Lauren, taking a bite as he sits. "I'm still so hungry," he adds, mumbling through his food.

Lauren takes a sip of her coffee and places her hand on Dek's arm. "We need to find some privacy where we can talk about what's going on with us before our meeting with Dr. Strong. We've been moving at such a fast pace, with little to no privacy, my head is spinning." She pauses, taking another sip of coffee. "My body's changing. I can feel it," she whispers, the strain showing in her eyes.

Taking time to finish his food, Dek covers her hand with his. "We'll figure this out, I promise," he reassures her, glancing past her across the street. "I was thinking about letting Richard in on our situation. What do you think?"

"Can you trust him? He seems weird and kind of slimy," she says, taking another sip of coffee.

"I've been lab partners with him for about six months now. We've never been friends, but he's smart and could maybe help us figure this thing out. That would also solve our privacy problem."

"Making him leave would solve that problem too," she replies. "I don't trust him. He acts very greed-driven, so he may try to sell us to the nearest carnival freakshow just to make a buck," she jokes, trying to keep the mood light.

"As long as we stay away from any carnivals looking for spare freaks, I believe we'll be okay," Decklan says with a smile. "I think it's worth a shot. Let's tell him a little and see how he responds, then we can decide if we should let him in on the meeting with Strong."

"Okay, he's starting to cross the street. What are we going to tell him? The hand or something else?" she says, sitting back in her chair.

"I'll take the lead, but interrupt if I start going the wrong direction," Dek whispers as Richard walks in, acknowledging them with a nod and going to the counter to order.

***

"So how was the important call?" Dek asks as Richard takes a seat across from the couple.

"It was my stepdad. He was giving me a hard time about staying at the school. He wants me on his research staff at his company, and he's been trying to get me on board since I graduated. He thinks a great brain like mine could be a real asset to his company," Richard lies through his teeth.

"Why don't you go?" Dek asks. "I'd kill to get a great research job with a big company. What does your dad's company do?"

Realizing his bragging may be getting him into trouble, Richard starts to backtrack. "My *step*dad is on the board of some chemical research company. They work with household-cleaning items. Boring stuff."

"What company is—" Lauren starts to ask but is cut off by Dek wanting to move on to the subject at hand.

"We've been talking, Richard, and we want to ask your scientific opinion on a problem that we've encountered since the accident," Dek starts, glancing at Lauren to make sure she's still on board with this.

"Sure, what kind of problem?" Richard responds eagerly.

"Ever since the accident, we've been experiencing some … side effects to the chemicals that we were exposed to in the hood. We want to test the filter to see if we can figure out what's going on."

"What kind of side effects?" asks Richard. "Headaches? Fatigue? Honestly, you guys look great."

"Well, that's just it. We're feeling better than great. Almost superhuman. All of our senses have improved, and we can hear better, see farther, and smell from a great distance," Dek cautiously explains. "My hand is healing at an accelerated rate, not to mention, any injury that I suffer is healing in minutes to hours. It almost feels like we've been upgraded."

Richard pauses, giving both of them a look. "You're saying that whatever you stumbled on in the lab has improved you?" he asks, sounding skeptical. "We're running down here to Dr. Strong because you guys feel *good* after the accident? What're you hoping to find in the filter? Some kind of miracle cure for whatever ails you?"

"I guess we're more worried that this will lead to some kind of cancer or something that starts off good and turns really bad," Dek says with a shrug.

"If you're going to let me in on this 'secret,' can I at least see your magically healing hand?" Richard asks, relieved they're not trying to steal any of the research. This is probably just some vast overreaction he can easily dispel, and then he can get back home.

Dek reaches down to undo the bandages on his hand when the guy sitting at the next table shifts his arm, knocking his full cup of coffee to the ground and spraying Richard's leg with the hot liquid. Dek and Lauren instinctively hop up and shift away from the mess as Richard yelps in pain, the coffee burning his leg and staining his expensive shoes. "Shit! What the hell, man?" he shouts as the man runs to grab some napkins.

"I'm so sorry!" he says, bending down to soak up the mess.

Lauren gets some towels and helps to clean the floor, handing some to Richard for his leg and shoes. Having been disrupted from the conversation, Dek tells Richard he'll show him his hand later at the meeting with Dr. Strong.

"You guys are letting me go?" Richard asks excitedly.

"I guess," Dek replies.

"Let's go and get set up with a hotel room," Lauren suggests as they walk to the car. "I'd like to get settled before we meet with Strong."

Though happy to be part of the meeting, Richard continues to sulk and complain about his shoes.

CHAPTER 10

At five o'clock that afternoon, the three of them meet Dr. Strong at his lab on the third floor of the bioengineering building. The lab is huge, with two separate testing areas and a glassed-in office at the center, and it contains a massive desk with a bank of computers behind it. The office reminds Dek of the car dealerships that had a glassed-in area over the sales floor where the salesman would ask the manager about a price reduction. There are four computer screens all synced to one keyboard. Dr. Strong is at the desk, sitting in a large, comfy chair, his back to them as he changes the placement of carbon atoms on a mockup of a chemical structure.

"Hey, doc," Lauren says as they enter through the open office door. "Still trying to manipulate the forces of nature to make the world a better place?"

"Miss Summers, so good to see you again! Just tinkering with a structure. You never know what you might find unless you try. So what can I do to help these budding minds of science?" he replies, rotating his chair to face them and shutting down his computer screen.

Closing the door for privacy, Dek and Lauren sit on some smaller, less-comfortable chairs across the desk while Richard remains standing, leaning against the back wall.

"Dr. Strong, as we mentioned at lunch, Dek and I both were involved in a lab accident about a week ago," Lauren begins, taking the lead and getting right to the point. "After the accident, we've been experiencing changes to our bodies. Just about everything is improved. Heightened senses, rapid healing, and increased endurance and cognitive functions."

"Can you give me some specific examples of these changes?" Strong asks, slightly intrigued but thinking they're greatly exaggerating the extent of their *changes*.

"Where do I start? I don't even need to wear glasses or contacts to see perfectly. Dek's hand was injured in the accident and has regrown two fingers in seven days. Cuts and bruises heal within minutes. We can adjust our vision to see in the dark. Dek went for a run and had the stamina, endurance, and speed of an Olympic athlete. These are just a few things we've noticed in the past week," Lauren explains, excited to finally be able to tell someone the crazy list of changes they've been encountering since the accident.

"You said that you've been on the run since the accident. Are you in some kind of trouble with the law?" Strong asks, not getting distracted by the list or letting them brush over any important information.

"We aren't really sure," Dek says honestly. He then tells Strong all about waking up in the hospital, investigating the lab with Lauren, and escaping the basement after the janitor locked them in the closet. When he finishes his rather long story, he sits back in his chair and takes a deep breath, looking for some kind of reaction from the professor.

Strong stares at them silently, thinking through all Dek had just explained. Rubbing his chin, he asks, "Miss Summers, what were you testing in this modified hood?"

"I was working for a private company and signed a nondisclosure agreement," she says, knowing Strong will know what that means and probably suspected as much when he asked her about it.

"Those types of agreements are super strict," Richard interjects, entering the conversation for the first time.

Strong looks at him questioningly and agrees, saying, "Yes, I know what those types of agreements mean. I also know that it's very likely the source of your accident. Mr. Thomas, you were working on some samples for a professor, correct? Do you think that these samples could have released anything toxic?"

Dek shakes his head. "I've done this sort of thing many times in the past few months and have never had a problem."

"Well then, Miss Summers, to correctly answer your question of why this accident occurred and what has caused the changes that you're describing, you will need to break your nondisclosure agreement," Strong says matter-of-factly.

"It's not fair to put her in that position," Richard says, kicking off the wall. "She could be sued by her employer."

"Judging by the extreme changes that she's experiencing, this could be life-threatening or even a health risk to herself and others. I think that it would stand up in court if it got that far. What were you doing, Lauren?" Strong asks, returning his focus to her.

"I was testing a type of rare radioactive metal to see the extent of the radioactive signature and how well the signature could be read through different materials. It was only first-stage testing. I'm sure my findings were only an indication to see if it could go on to further, more in-depth tests for its true use."

"You don't have to say anything more!" Richard rudely interjects. "This could hurt your long-term career goals."

"It's okay, Richard. Strong's right. If this is serious, I could be dead soon or become some kind of Typhoid Mary. I think that's more important than my career," Lauren replies.

Strong is silent and stone-faced as he runs his hands through his white hair. "Did you take proper precautions and use appropriate safety measures while working with this material? I didn't think that those types of tests were approved for that kind of setting."

"I used every precaution that I could, including modifying the hood, which may have allowed for the accident to occur," Lauren admits, looking away from Dek.

For the first time, she has taken some responsibility for the accident. She was always hiding behind the nondisclosure agreement to avoid telling Dek why the hood had taken off part of his hand. She'd been doing experiments that weren't approved and removing safety features from the hood that would've stopped the shield from smashing his hand.

Dek shakes his head, holding his injured hand. "You were letting me believe that it was *my samples* that caused the accident," he says, seething with utter disappointment.

"I'm sorry," she whispers, still refusing to look at him. "I really hoped that it was your samples, but I knew that I had tampered with the equipment and was, at least, partly at fault."

"'Partly at fault'?" he exclaims. "I could've been maimed for life or killed!"

"You shouldn't have even been there in the first place!" she yells back, turning sharply to face him. "That wasn't your lab, and the door was locked. How was I supposed to know that you were planning to break in and use my equipment?"

Before things get out of control, Dr. Strong interjects, saying, "You *both* acted irresponsibly, causing the accident. Now you need to focus on finding a solution to your problem and stop trying to assign blame."

"Yes, you're right," Dek says, slightly lowering his head. "I'm sorry, Lauren. We need to work together to figure this out."

"I'm sorry too," she says, taking his injured hand.

"Look, this is all great," Richard interjects. "We're spilling some company's secret study information and hashing out who's to blame. Both of you seem to be all right, so why are we even bothering Dr. Strong?"

"Because of this," Dek says, unwrapping his bandage to show two pale but fully healed fingers, which he can now move and feel again less than a week later.

Lauren leans back as Richard comes forward to look at Dek's hand, and Strong walks around his desk to take a closer look. Palpitating the two fingers, Strong whispers, "Amazing." Then he returns to his seat without saying another word. He gently rubs his forehead, as he does when he ponders a puzzling situation. After a minute, he mumbles to himself, "This is big. This could be a turning point in medical history. Not only did we have this miraculous regrowth hidden somewhere in our DNA, but we also have the fact that Miss Summers was affected as well and has experienced similar remarkable side effects due to the accident." Pausing again to regain his thoughts, he continues, "I'm not sure that we should keep this secret. I'm not really qualified to take on medical research like this."

Before he gets too carried away, Richard interjects again. "We need to keep this secret until we know more about it. The way the media is, this could blow up into a widescale panic. Dek and Lauren could be taken away and experimented on, like medical guinea pigs! This is *not* the sort of thing that you can reveal without having a better understanding of how it works. We don't even have the samples that caused this. Other than these two and their story, we don't have much to go on without further testing."

"I think Richard could be right," Dek says. "What if this is just the first stage of some kind of cancer? I've never heard of rapid cell growth like this before."

"Okay, this is a lot to digest," Strong says. "I suggest that we all go home and sleep on it. We'll plan to meet back here first thing in the morning and decide the best plan of action. Let's agree not to talk to anyone outside of this group until then."

The trio nods in agreement and thanks Dr. Strong for his help.

"Of course," he says. "I'm happy to be part of your journey. Hopefully, we'll be able to come to an appropriate decision."

***

The trio return to the hotel in relative silence. Lauren and Dek go to their separate beds to lie down while Richard sits on the sofa, just staring at a blank TV screen and trying to process all that was revealed today.

Twenty minutes later, Dek and Lauren are woken up by Lauren's buzzing phone. "Strong's delaying us," she says after she checks her messages.

"What?" Richard asks, his thoughts still spinning.

Lauren holds up her phone with a shrug. "He just texted me. Apparently, he's got an impromptu college staff meeting tomorrow. On the bright side, I have a great idea for us to burn a day. Don't plan on sleeping in."

"Sorry, I'm out," Richard says, shaking his head. "One of my professors needs help grading some papers. I can do it on my laptop from here, but it may take all day."

"We'll find a way to manage without you," says Dek with a smile, figuring Lauren didn't actually intend to include Richard in her "great idea."

"Anyway, I'm going to get some shuteye. What a crazy day," Richard says, reclining on the couch.

At 3 a.m., Dek is startled by Lauren climbing into his bed. "Can't sleep?" he whispers as she snuggles into his chest. The smell of her hair is intoxicating.

"Scared. I just hate not knowing what's going to happen. Could you just hold me?" she asks, pulling his arms tight around her.

"Sure," he says with a reassuring squeeze.

CHAPTER 11

Lauren gently nudges Dek awake the next morning. "Time to wake up, big guy. I told you I wasn't going to let you sleep in."

He sits up on the edge of the bed, stretching out his arms. "So, what's the plan for today?" he asks with a yawn.

"Today, you'll have a feast for the senses! We're going on a sense-stimulating tour of Lake Shore Chicago," she says excitedly. "We're going to test the limits of our heightened senses and tour the city. Get ready to stroll and sightsee in the name of science."

Dek gives her a meager smile and thumbs-up as she exits the room to allow him time to dress. He must admit, he's very excited to spend some alone time with Lauren and enjoys seeing her happy, especially considering how stressed she's been this past week.

They leave a sleeping Richard on the couch and exit the hotel, feeling a brisk wind whipping past the doorway and catching a whiff of flowers and freshly cut grass. "May get some rain today," Lauren says, looking up at the partly cloudy sky. "Most summer afternoons, we'll get a stray pop-up shower."

Dek takes her hand. "So where are we off to, Summers?"

"Our first stop is a must for anyone visiting Chicago: a ride on the L Red Line."

They walk about three blocks to the nearest Red Line stop. The L is an elevated train that serves as public transportation to downtown Chicago. They walk up to the rundown platform, colorful graffiti decorating the sides, to get on the train.

Lauren picks two seats near the middle. "Okay," she starts. "This is the start of our first senses challenge. Please keep looking at me and not around the train."

"Not a problem," Dek says with a wry smile.

"We're going to use the people on the L to test our sense of smell. Close your eyes and concentrate on picking up the smells around you and see how far down the train car you can identify the people sitting behind you. What they do or something unique about them. I'll do the same. We'll see who's more correct and accurate the farther back we go."

"Okay, but how will we judge this?" he asks, excited for a challenge.

"I'll look over your shoulder, and you can look over mine. A lot of people are going to and from work, so we should have lots to work with. I'll go first," she says, closing her eyes. "I've got a cleaning woman about five seats back. A strong scent of bleach. Probably coming home from work. I can pick up a faint after-work body odor, as well as a waning smell of perfume."

Dek looks over her shoulder, and sure enough, about five seats back, there's a gray-haired woman in a white cleaning outfit. Based on the tired look on her face, she does appear to be done with her day. "Yep, point for you," Dek says as Lauren opens her eyes. "My turn." He closes his eyes and takes a big whiff. "About seven seats back, I've got a doctor or medical worker. There's a strong scent of hand sanitizer that's commonly used in hospitals."

Lauren looks past him. "They're wearing scrubs, so I'll give it to you. My turn again."

They go back and forth for a while, the occasional stops mixing up the smells as people enter and exit the train. They're tied points-wise, but Lauren is currently winning distance-wise. "We're almost at our stop. One more chance to overtake my distance," she says, smiling victoriously.

Decklan closes his eyes again and concentrates on the smells coming from behind him. He's come to realize that the more he focuses on this one task, the better it seems to work. "I got one," he says. "This has got to be near the last seat in the car. Probably a cop or member of law enforcement. I can smell gunpowder. Very faint ... maybe hidden under a jacket or shirt."

Lauren looks to the back as the train pulls up to the stop. A man in a bulky coat is sitting where Dek said, but he doesn't look like a cop. In fact, he seems to be paying too much attention to an older woman Dek ID'd earlier in the game. As the train pulls to a stop, she gets up, and the man mimics her. "Oh, shit, Dek I think something's going down," Lauren says, jumping to her feet and hurrying down the car, pushing past people before the doors can open. "Aunt Sophie!" she yells as she nears the woman, drawing everyone's attention.

The man immediately backs off and exits as the doors open.

Dek comes in behind Lauren as she says to the woman, "Oh, I'm so sorry. You look just like my aunt." She then turns back to Dek. "This is our stop. Roosevelt."

As they step off the train, Dek asks, "What the hell was that?"

"I think that man was going to snatch her purse or something," Lauren explains. "So I pretended to know her to draw attention and scare him off."

"Wow, you're like a real superhero," Dek teases, earning an elbow in the side. "Seriously, though. That was cool, the way you handled that situation."

"Thanks. Now let's take a stroll through Grant Park."

It doesn't take long for them to reach the north side of the large urban park located within the central business district of downtown Chicago. It's highlighted by the picturesque Buckingham Fountain and the Art Institute of Chicago and bustling with other walkers and tourists.

Wanting to continue testing their senses, they decide to focus on their hearing as they walk for about fifteen minutes, trying to identify the many sounds of the park. There are a lot of birds in the park but not much variety. In the end, they find themselves talking more than listening, just enjoying their time together.

Suddenly, Dek stops walking and looks over as a short, Black man in a blue windbreaker gets up and leaves a nearby park bench.

"What's up?" Lauren asks, following his line of sight toward the man who's now walking away.

"Have you noticed that some people's bodies are making a sound?" he whispers, pulling her closer.

"Yeah ... it's almost like a buzzing or humming sound, but it only comes from a few people. Most people's bodies are pretty quiet," she replies, still watching the man.

"That guy was humming so loud that it drew my attention. I guess maybe it's just because I'm trying so hard to focus on my hearing."

"To be honest, you make the same sound," she says, looking up at him. "How about me?"

"You do too, but not as loud as *that* guy. I wonder what it is ...? I hope we aren't hearing the blood rushing past plaque in our arteries or something crazy like that," he says, now slightly worried.

When they exit the park, they walk up the huge stairs leading to the Field Museum. Inside, Lauren makes Dek look at every plaque they pass during their walk through the exhibits.

Leaving the museum, Lauren takes Dek back toward the loop section of downtown Chicago to a nice restaurant with an outside terrace for lunch.

"Okay, Supergirl, what's next on our feast for the senses?" Dek asks before downing a slice of pepperoni pizza.

"While you eat, I want you to think back on the plaques that we read in the museum and write down on your napkin as many of the dates that you can recall. Just the dates, not the significance," she says as she hands him a pen from her bag, grabbing one for herself. They spread out their napkins and start to write in between bites. After about ten minutes and finishing off a whole Chicago-style pizza, Lauren says, "Time's up. What've you got?"

They line up their napkins side-by-side and realize they have the exact same list of dates in the order they saw them in the museum. "That's crazy," Decklan says, taking a final drink of his cola.

"I had a feeling that this would be the result," Lauren says. "I know I didn't ask for you to write it down, but do you remember the significance of the dates?"

"I think so," Dek says in disbelief. "How can that be? I generally have a good memory, but this is taking it over the top. How did you know this would be the result?"

"I've been able to recall almost everything that's happened since the accident with remarkable clarity. I'm not sure what's going on with us, but for the most part, it's been very positive and exciting."

"Maybe ... until we find out that we're actually dying of some rare disease."

"Thanks, Dek, way to look on the bright side. Are you ready to finish off our tour?"

"Let's do it," he replies, getting up from the table.

Lauren takes a second to watch him as he cleans up some of the crumbs around his plate. He somehow seems so carefree and positive after all they've been through. *I don't know how I would ever be able to do this without his emotional support*, she thinks as she gets up and crosses the table, giving him a little kiss on the cheek.

"Wow, what was that for?" he asks her with a smile.

"Being a good companion," she replies, taking his hand.

They walk a couple of blocks farther down the street and arrive at the Willis Tower. Pausing to look up at the mammoth building as it climbs to the sky, Dek says, "This better be a sight test and not a flight test."

"You're correct," Lauren says with a laugh, taking his hand and leading him inside. "But you gotta admit, flight would be pretty cool." They ride the elevator up to the observation deck, a large room with some benches for people with vertigo and walls of giant glass windows overlooking the city from every direction. "Okay, close your eyes and focus your thoughts on maximizing your vision—much like we were able to adjust our vision in the dark storage room. This time, focus on distance," Lauren instructs. "When I tell you to open your eyes, try to look for the farthest thing that you can make out clearly, and we'll compare our results."

Standing next to each other at the guard rails, they both close their eyes for a minute, then Lauren says, "Okay, open." Then they look out the window.

They choose to face the side of the building that looks out over the land rather than the lakeside because there should be a variety of things to see.

"Wow," says Dek, slowly peering out over the city. "It feels like I can see forever. I can't believe the clarity and detail, even at this distance. I don't think I'd be able to see this well if I put a quarter in one of those telescope machines."

"I can easily see the airport and make out the insignias on the planes on the runway," Lauren says, drawing Dek's attention back to the game.

"Yeah, I can see it," he says, looking in the same direction. "The plane that's just about to take off. Little girl with brown pigtails in the—"

"Third window!" Lauren interrupts. "Yes, wow, I can't believe the distance. I feel like they're right here in front of me."

"This must be how a hawk feels as it circles high above a field and spots a small mouse from miles away. I guess we can officially call it a draw," Dek says, turning back toward the interior of the observation deck. "The other crazy thing is how quickly my eyes adjusted back once I turned from the window," he comments as they walk back to the elevator.

As the elevator doors open, Lauren adds with a laugh, "Last chance to test that flying idea."

"I think I'll try leaping tall buildings with a single bound first," Dek retorts. "It's getting close to four-thirty. Should we head back to the hotel?" he asks as they return to the street, checking his watch.

"Wait, Deck, look! Is that the same guy we saw earlier on the L? The guy with the gun who was stalking that old lady?" Lauren says, pointing across the street.

Dek looks in the direction she's pointing. "Yeah, I think it is. He's heading back up toward the platform, maybe looking for another target."

"That's it, I need to have a word with this jerk," Lauren says, hurrying after the man before Dek can stop her. She quickly catches up to the man just as he reaches the platform. "Sir? Sir!" she says, getting his attention and making a small scene. "Don't think I can't see just what you're doing. You know, people on this train want to ride safely without the threat of being mugged or assaulted, so why don't you knock it off?"

"Look, lady, you got the wrong idea," the guy says with a heavy Chicago accent.

"Don't you think the other passengers on this train should know you're carrying a gun?" Lauren blurts out, causing Dek to face-palm.

The man takes a closer look at Lauren, shocked she's alerting all the passengers on the waiting deck he has a gun. "Wait a minute … it's you!" he says, taken aback. "You're the lady who was helping that pickpocket on the train earlier. Ma'am, you may not realize this, but I'm an undercover train security officer. I was trailing that woman until you stepped in with that 'hey aunty' routine. Are you working with her, trying to out me in front of all the passengers?"

"Oh, shit," Dek says over a humiliated Lauren's shoulder. "We're so sorry, officer. We saw you following that woman and thought you were going to rob her, not the other way around."

"But how do you know I'm carrying a gun?" the cop asks, lowering his voice and cautiously looking around to see if the other passengers are still paying attention.

"I-I could smell the gunpowder on you," Lauren stammers out of shock.

He sniffs his jacket and says, "I don't smell anything, but maybe I'm just used to it. Listen, you guys need to leave the police work to the police, okay? Thanks for trying to be good citizens, but it can

be very dangerous if you're not trained to handle such situations."
He then turns to get on the departing train.

Dek looks down at Lauren. "I guess we can just get the next
train. It might be awkward being on the same train with him
again."

"God, I feel so stupid," Lauren says. "I could've sworn I picked
up such a weird vibe from him earlier. Maybe it was because he was
being deceitful by hiding his identity as a cop."

"Maybe ... did you notice that his body was also making that
same humming sound? What if you just picked up on that?"

"Could be, I guess."

***

As they exit the L and begin the short walk back to the hotel, Dek
says, "I had a really good time hanging out with you today."

"Yeah, it was fun," Lauren replies, a little distracted. "I just
can't shake the feeling that the cop guy was up to something that
had nothing to do with police work. I was so sure ...."

"Even superheroes get it wrong sometimes," Dek says as they
arrive at the hotel.

They both say hi to Richard, who's reading a book before bed,
as they enter their room and take turns showering to wash off the
sweat of the day.

Hours later, Dek isn't as surprised as he was the previous night
when Lauren climbs into his bed and snuggles against him.

"Would you mind a little company?" she asks knowingly.

"Sounds like a great way to end a great day," he whispers,
wrapping his arms around her.

"God, you're corny."

CHAPTER 12

The next morning, Dek wakes up around 6 a.m., realizing Lauren's already gone. Her smell on the sheets reminds him of the way spending time with her makes him feel. She seems to be setting a new record of him sleeping with a woman and not having sex with her, and he's not so sure how long that trend is going to last. His heightened senses make him very aware of every sexual signal a nearby woman gives off. He can now pick up abundant pheromones, increased heartbeats, pupil dilation, or intense blushing almost unconsciously. It's a little intense for a man who was already aware of the opposite sex.

He's pulled out of his sexual reverie when he sees Richard typing away on his laptop.

Richard perks up when Dek sits up. "Hey, Dek, did you get lucky last night?" he quips, feeling like he has some inside info having seen Lauren leave Dek's bed earlier that morning.

"Sorry, bud, a gentleman doesn't kiss and tell," Dek says with a grin. "Do you know where Lauren is?" Dek asks, grabbing a diet cola from the fridge. The sun is starting to come up, and he can feel the need to bathe in its rays.

"Don't you already know, lover boy?" Richard chimes from the couch.

Dek gets the impression Richard's not used to having roommates, especially ones who have sleepovers with women. His attempts to deal with the situation are starting to get annoying. "Look, Richard, my relationship with Lauren is none of your business, and I need you to stop making crude comments about it before I lose my cool. Got it?"

"Yeah, sorry, man," Richard apologizes sheepishly. "I'm just really excited about today. I know we didn't talk much about it yesterday, but I've been searching the web, and there are definitely rare cases of people growing back part of a lost limb but nothing like what you showed us with your hand and nothing at that speed."

"We'll see what Strong thinks," Dek says, getting up as Lauren comes into the room, dressed in black yoga capris and a turquoise sports bra. Her hair is tied back in a ponytail, revealing a sexy neck. "Sun's coming up. Are you up for a run?" she asks, taking Dek's breath away.

"S-sure," he stammers. "You look ready to challenge the champ."

He quickly changes and meets her downstairs in the lobby. Stepping off the elevator, he sees Lauren stretching in the sun just outside the door. The desk clerk can barely pull his eyes away from her long enough to say, "Good morning."

She does look fantastic.

Dek steps outside, soaking in the sun's warmth on his skin and taking in a deep breath of fresh air. The sightseeing tour of the lakefront the day before took all day, and the sun was waning when they finished. Now, Dek's body is instantly recharged. "You're going to cause the desk clerk to have a heart attack if you keep stretching out here," he says jokingly.

"I was hoping to have that effect on you," she teases back, flirtatiously peeking over her shoulder and giving him a wink.

Dek clears his throat and runs a sweaty hand through his hair. "We'd better get going before my hormones kick into overdrive," he replies, taking off before she finishes her stretch to get a little lead. "Come on, slowpoke!"

They run for about thirty minutes, trying to push their limits. They then stop to cool down about a block from the hotel.

"I can see what you meant the other day," Lauren says, catching her breath. "I haven't run like that in years, and I was keeping up with you pretty well. I can feel my muscles and tendons responding to my need. I think my leg muscles have doubled in size, pulling in more water to keep up with demand. My knee also feels great. In the past, if I ran even a little, I would have to ice it for half an hour and have a limp for a few days because of the pain. We'll have to see how well I recover from this little jog."

"Yeah, I noticed it too. Not to mention your great-looking glutes," Dek teases.

"Is that why you let me take the lead so many times? To check out my glutes?" she asks, smiling.

"Guilty as charged," he replies, enjoying the sexual banter. "I found the other day that my legs returned to normal quickly after a few minutes of walking. It feels like I have greater control over how my body reacts to situations and needs."

"If my glutes don't start returning to normal size, I'll never fit in my pants," Lauren jokes, patting her butt.

Thirty minutes later, they return to the hotel room, shower, and change into lab-appropriate clothes to meet with Dr. Strong at 10 a.m. Richard waits for them with some bagels he got from the store, impatiently tapping his foot. They each finish off a bagel and leave at 9:45 a.m., eager to continue the day.

***

As Dek, Lauren, and Richard pull out of the hotel garage, a black sedan pulls away from the curb and follows them, careful to keep its distance until they enter the biochem parking lot. The car passes by the lab and returns to the hotel. There, Mr. Vincent exits the car and takes the elevator to the fourth floor. Finding Room 435, he uses a passkey to crack the door's lock and slips inside. After determining the kids took the filter with them to the lab, he places a mic in a discrete location to listen in on their conversations. He then takes a seat in the chair beside the TV at a small desk and dials a number in his cell phone.

"Do you have good news for us?" Feldman answers coldly after two rings.

"I'm sitting in their room as we speak. They took the filter with them. Richard insists that he has everything under control and that they're not after our research project."

"Don't trust that idiot!" Feldman angrily shouts through the speaker. "This situation needs to be cleaned up soon. We're moving forward with second-level tests, and they're looking very promising. We don't need any undue publicity ruining this deal."

"I understand. To what degree do you want the situation handled?"

"All persons with any knowledge of the samples we're testing could be a risk to the project. I expect that you'll handle the situation with your normal amount of professionalism and discretion," Feldman replies before hanging up.

Mr. Vincent sits back in the chair for a minute. With a small, knowing smile, he gets up and heads for the door.

CHAPTER 13

The trio enters the lab to find Dr. Strong buzzing around, like a trapped bee bouncing from station to station. There are two lab assistants—a tall, athletic-looking guy with short, cropped, brown hair and a small, attractive girl with streaked, blond hair pulled back in a ponytail—wearing white coats and sitting at a table, writing furiously on their clipboards.

Strong stops working when he spots the three grad students. "Hey, good morning!" he half-yells, clearly excited to begin the day's experiments. "Did you get enough sleep? Have you had some breakfast? We have bagels if you're hungry," he rattles off.

"I think we're ready to go," Dek says with some apprehension, eyeing the two lab techs.

"Oh, yes," Strong says, momentarily forgetting they were there. "This is Bobby Williams and Stacy Mills. They'll be helping with recording the data and setting everything up. Bobby is a physical therapy grad student, and Stacy is one of my grad students here. Bobby will do more of the physical testing, taking down what you're athletically capable of doing, and Stacy will help me with the medical side of the tests."

Seeing a slightly worried look on Dek's face, Strong quickly adds, "Don't worry. I've worked with them both since they started school at Northwestern, and I trust both of them with the confidentiality needed in this case."

"All right, Strong," Dek says with a slight nod of the head. "How do we begin?"

"That's the spirit!" Strong exclaims. "I want Lauren to go with Bobby. He's set up some physical tests for you in the east gym, which we commonly use for experiments. Decklan, you'll stay here. I want to get some bloodwork and an X-ray of that damaged hand, as well as some tissue samples. Sound good?"

"I guess I'll catch you later then," Dek says to Lauren as she and Bobby leave for the gym. "Richard, are you staying here for the science stuff or running off for the wide world of sports?" he asks, looking back over his shoulder.

"Science is my thing, but the feats of strength sound more interesting. I'll catch you later, man," Richard says, chasing after Bobby and Lauren.

***

It's about a two-block walk to the east gym, and Lauren peels off her large T-shirt, showing off her tight, pink spaghetti strap tanktop and spandex athlete shorts. Letting the sun warm her skin, she puts her hair in a lazy bun and stretches her arms and back as she walks. "So how long have you worked with Dr. Strong, Bobby?" she asks just as Richard jogs up to join them.

"Hey, guys, mind if I tag along?" he asks, trying to catch his breath.

"Glad to have the extra hands," Bobby says. Turning his attention back to Lauren, he adds, "I've been helping Dr. Strong for about four years, ever since I took his biochem class my sophomore year. He has an amazing mind. You picked a good person to help you with your experiment. Now, he hasn't told me everything, just that I need to test you athletically and test your reflexology. Are you trying out for some kind of pro sports team?"

Lauren bites the inside of her cheek to keep herself from laughing. "I'm actually a scientist, but I'm glad you think I look like an athlete. This is more to test the limitations of some supplements I'm trying out for a manufacturer," she says, glancing back at Richard and signaling him with her eyes to go along with her story. She feels it'll be best to keep Bobby in the dark until Strong wants to let him in on the true nature of the tests.

"Are these supplements like vitamins or amino acids?" Bobby asks.

"Something like that," Lauren replies mysteriously. "It's kind of hush-hush until the company's ready to release the findings of the tests."

"I would think that the company would do that testing in their own labs if it was so secret," Bobby pries, trying to get through Lauren's bull and giving her a knowing look.

"I often do some private tests that companies don't want on their official logbooks until they have a better idea of what the test results will be," Lauren adds, swiftly deflecting Bobby's skepticism.

They arrive at the east gym, and Bobby uses a key to let them in through the side door. "Looks like it's all ours today," he says, holding open the door for them and not-so-subtly bragging about his exclusive access to school property.

The gym is set up like an NFL training combine. One side is lined with bleachers overlooking a large expanse of purple, parquet flooring. Tests to measure speed, agility, and strength are positioned in different stations. The ceiling has a row of dirty, old windows, allowing in some outdoor light in addition to the fluorescent yellow glow of the gym lighting.

"Take a few minutes to stretch, then we can begin," Bobby says, already jotting down some notes and pre-workout measurements on his clipboard.

As he sets up next to the vertical jump station, Lauren sits down and stretches her legs, concentrating on her thighs and calves. After a few minutes, she pops up and jogs over to Bobby. "Jump up and hit the bars?" she asks, crouching down to jump.

"You got it," he says, standing with a stick to reset the bars after she tries. "I left it pretty high, so you may not be able to get any."

Amused, Lauren jumps up and knocks away about half of the bars. Glancing over at the guys, she says, "I'm just warming up. Let me try again." She then pops back up and knocks away another five bars.

"I can't believe it. That's incredible!" Bobby exclaims, no longer doubting the little scientist's athletic ability. "You have to be about five foot five, and you touched at nine foot eight. That's crazy! Your vertical is about two-and-a-half feet."

"With a little practice, I bet I could do even better," Lauren says with a big smile. "What's next?"

"How about the forty-yard dash?" Richard suggests, seeing that Bobby's still a little stunned by the vertical jump.

"All right," Lauren says, running over to the starting line. "Is this where I start?" she asks, getting into a runner's stance.

"Hold on," Bobby says, jogging to the finish line. "Let me get my stopwatch ready." After a few clicks, he says, "On your mark, get set, go!"

Lauren isn't a sprinter and is a hair late on the start but finishes in 4.5 seconds. She then jogs back around to a wide-eyed Bobby.

"That's near Olympic training speed," he says. "People don't just walk out of the science lab and run like that. What kind of supplements are you testing?"

"Can't say. Where to next?" Lauren says, jogging in place to stay warmed up.

"Try the weights," Richard replies.

"Lemme at 'em!" Lauren growls, giving a dramatic flexing pose.

The testing goes on for about an hour. The time consists of a stunned Bobby, an excited Richard, and an enthusiastic Lauren running from test to test like a bunny on speed. She finally starts to tire after the long jump and shuttle run. Taking a break, she downs a giant glass of water and rests on the bleachers. "Everything's going great, but I feel like I'm missing something."

"'Going great' might be the understatement of the year," Bobby says. "If you could pass a drug test with this supplement you're on, you could be in the next Olympics. It's some kind of steroids or HGH, isn't it? I need to get a few post-workout muscle measurements, and then we can go."

"It's not steroids, and I can't tell you any more about it at this time," Lauren says firmly. "When I ran with Dek this morning, I didn't seem to tire at all, and that was a similarly stressful workout. Now, I feel my energy draining. What's different?"

"Maybe it's because you have a thing for Dek," Richard unhelpfully chimes in with a mocking tone. "You had a burst of hormones."

"Competition can make your workout harder," Bobby adds, ignoring Richard's immaturity. "Is Decklan taking the same supplements?"

"Similar," Lauren says as Bobby measures her calf and thigh circumference. "But I don't think that's it."

"Okay, I'm done here," Bobby says, glancing over the data on his clipboard. "We have some great numbers. I can't wait to show Strong. You have almost a half-inch gain in thigh and calf muscle size. You seem to be able to get the blood and muscle to respond at will. You have great circulation. Strong said to expect something good, but you were *amazing.*"

"Thanks," Lauren replies, slightly embarrassed by all the attention. "I think that may be the first time in my athletic life that I've been referred to as 'amazing.' I've had 'not bad' and 'better luck next time' but rarely, if ever, 'amazing.'"

As the three exit the gym, the guys quickly raise their hands, shielding their face as the bright sunlight stings their eyes. "Wow, I forgot what a difference it is going from the gym's lights to sunlight," Richard says, looking back at the door.

Lauren's the only one affected differently. She stares up at the sun, opening her arms to embrace its glow. "It's the sun," she says, lowering her arms.

"Yeah, it took a scientist to figure that one out, huh?" Richard snaps, walking a few steps ahead.

"No, you idiot, the sun is what was missing from the workout. I feel like a million bucks now just from walking outside and feeling it on my skin. The sun seems to react, somehow, with the changes in my body. It's refueling me," she says emphatically. "I can almost feel my cells refueling and healing my muscle tissue." She crouches down and explodes in a vertical jump, touching the side of the wall that's at least six inches higher than what she reached inside the gym.

"How can you do that after the workout you just did?" Bobby asks, stunned.

"The sun," Lauren repeats triumphantly. "It has to be the key to this whole mystery. Let's get back to the lab. I *have* to share this with Dek!"

CHAPTER 14

As soon as Lauren and the guys exit the lab, Dr. Strong motions Dek to have a seat in a small chair with an arm support attached. "First thing's first," he says. "We'll need about three vials of blood. I want to look at cell structure, do DNA sequencing, and test your blood for infections and cancer markers. Luckily, I can do these tests here at the lab. I'll also need you to go over to the hospital for an X-ray of that hand. I have a research agreement with them, so they should do it for free. If it's healing as you say, we need to see what's going on in there. We may also need an MRI to get a better image of the muscle healing. When you get back, we'll hook you up to a brain scan and see if you have any extra brain activity since you feel these changes in your senses. It's going to be a long day of tests. Then we can all sit down and look over our data and discuss a hypothesis for what's happened to you."

Dek just sits back in his little chair, feeling like a parent sitting in a preschool classroom chair, and says, "Sounds good. Let's get started." Watching Strong take control of the testing gives Dek a real sense that they're working with the right people.

Stacy quickly gets three vials of blood from Dek. He's always had good veins, so it only takes a few minutes. Strong takes the vials to begin his tests, and Stacy leads Dek downstairs to her car for a quick ride to the hospital for his hand X-ray. Dek plops down in the passenger side of her Lexus sedan. "Nice car. I don't know many students who're driving a Lexus."

"I'm in grad school, and I make a decent amount of money on the side by helping out researchers like Dr. Strong, but my parents bought me the car as a graduation gift. They weren't too happy when I decided to stay in school for my master's. I think they wanted me to go out and find a rich man to settle down and have children with."

"I can't seem to pull myself away from school either. Maybe it's just that feeling of comfort in not taking on all the responsibility of an adult," he says.

"So Strong said you got hurt in a lab accident. Is that going to hurt your standing with the college?"

"I don't know. I hope not. This thing is getting way out of hand—no pun intended. I'm not sure my life will ever be the same," he says, pausing as they pull into the hospital parking garage a few minutes later. "Though, I'm not sure if I really want it to be."

They pull into a faculty parking spot and walk to the elevators. "Quick trip to the X-ray room, and we should be done in no time," Stacy says reassuringly.

* * *

It only takes a few minutes to shoot the X-ray and get the films developed.

"How does it look?" Dek asks as they walk back to the car.

"I'm not sure," she says. "I'll wait for Dr. Strong to take a look before I make any judgments. It's definitely a hand though," she adds with a smile, trying to lighten the mood.

They drive back to the lab in relative silence. Dek can't wait to see the X-ray. He's eager to see what has Stacy so perplexed. His hand is feeling better every day, and just being outside for the short car ride makes Dek feel recharged.

They barely get inside the lab before Strong starts asking them for the X-rays. He quickly puts them up on a reading lightboard as Stacy and Dek gather behind him.

"It's definitely a hand," Dek repeats jokingly, glancing at Stacy.

"Yes, Decklan, it does appear to be a fully functioning hand," Strong confirms, rubbing his chin as he stares at the X-ray. "The thing that bothers me is that the bones of the hand and even the wrist look whiter than the bones of the arm."

"I noticed it too," Stacy adds. "What do you make of it?"

"I would guess that it's indicating a thickening of the bone. This is sometimes seen in bone cancer where the bone cells are multiplying and thickening the bone wall. Assuming that the existing bone cells are generating new bone cells to heal the part of the hand that was crushed in the accident, it would be reasonable to have a similar thickening of the surrounding bones as they generate the new bone. It looks like a form of controlled cell reproduction rather than *un*controlled cell multiplication found in cancer."

"That can't be possible," Dek says. "I've never heard of anything like this before."

"I agree, it would definitely be a first," Strong says, glancing back at them. "Stacy, I need you to call the hospital in Madison that treated Decklan after the accident and request a copy of the X-rays they would've done when he was first brought in. Tell them that he's down here, receiving additional therapy and rehab services."

"Yes, sir," Stacy says before retreating to the desk to make the call.

"While she's doing that, I would like to put you through a computer program to test your cognitive abilities. This program will monitor your memory and problem solving, as well as give us an IQ reading," Strong says, leading Dek to a desk in the corner of the lab. "Have you ever done a test like this before?" he asks, pulling out the chair for him.

"I think I did something like this for a sociology class freshman year, but it's been a while."

"Let yourself go and relax. We want the truest measure of any cognitive enhancements that may have resulted from the accident. It's not like a school test; there are no penalties if you don't do well.

I'll give you some space while I go and check on Stacy. It should take you about an hour to finish."

Dek has taken this sort of test before, though it's not his favorite thing to do. In school, he always hated taking standardized tests. He reaches over and cracks the window shades, letting in a little light, and gets to work.

As he goes through the questions, he finds he can remember every question and every answer he's read. This is the first time in weeks he's tried to do anything like read, study, or take a test. His mind is reacting to his needs, just like his body did during his morning run, giving him the ability to read the questions quickly and figure out the answers in seconds. His excitement grows the more he works, and he finishes the test in just twenty-five minutes. He leans back in his chair, confidently announcing he's finished, only to realize Strong has taken over Stacy's call with the hospital and is very upset with something they're telling him on the phone.

Dek walks over to where the two of them are sitting at Strong's desk. "What's going on?" he whispers to Stacy who just shakes her head.

Then Strong yells at the poor guy on the other end of the phone, "This is a terrible failure in record keeping. I should report this to the board of medicine!" He pauses, listening to whomever he's speaking with ramble off some excuse. "Yes, please let me know when you've located the file. Thank you." Slamming the phone back on the receiver, Strong turns to Dek, his face red with anger. "I can't believe that a medical facility could act so negligently. They've lost all records of your injury—all X-rays, files, and notes. All gone. The only way I could confirm that you were even there was by talking to the nurse who had you as a patient. They're scrambling around, trying to recover the files so they can bill your insurance. They said they've been trying to get a hold of you as well. To be honest, with the way that your hand has healed, they'll be hard-pressed to even prove that the accident occurred or that you were there at all."

"Damn ... I can't believe they lost *all* those records. I guess I haven't been checking my messages lately," Dek says in disbelief.

"Were you injured any other times in the past few years that would have required an X-ray?" Strong asks.

"Yeah, in May of 2010, I cracked the small bone in my shin while playing softball. I know they took some X-rays of that injury."

"Let's try this again, Stacy. See if you can track down any of those records. Were you at the same hospital, Dek?"

"No, it was an urgent care place in Sun Prairie. Dr. Boswell treated me on ... I think it was May 5th, 2010, and the nurse's name was Shannon. Wow, after doing that cognitive work on the computer, my memory's working in overdrive."

"Are you already done?" Strong asks, shocked. "I thought you were just distracted by all my shouting on the phone. You were barely on there for thirty minutes. You can't be done yet." He quickly walks over to the station where Dek was testing.

"All done," Dek says proudly. "It was a snap."

Strong sits down and punches in some codes to get the results of the test. Shaking his head in amazement, he says, "You got all the answers correct. I don't think I've ever seen anything like this before. You finished in record time and got all the answers correct." He turns his chair around to face Dek, completely dumbfounded. "How did you do that?"

Dek just shrugs. "I'm honestly not really sure. When in doubt, just pick C," he jokes before getting serious again. "I can remember every question and answer that I put, and each one seemed correct. I can pull information from my memory like I'm looking it up on the computer. The test just helped me to focus on what I was trying to recall. If I really focus, things come back to me at an alarming rate, even old memories I'd forgotten a long time ago."

Strong remains silent as he processes the magnitude of what Dek is telling him. Finally, he says, "If you can recall all your memories and everything that you've read or learned, like a photographic memory, your capacity to learn would be off the charts. You could be the smartest person in the world. The trick to gaining intelligence is retaining what you've learned." He pauses again.

Dek just stands there, waiting for Strong to voice what he's thinking. He's clearly blown Strong's mind. He can almost see the wheels turning in Strong's head as he thinks up their next move.

"We need to get you strapped in for that brain scan," Strong says, decidedly raising his finger. "Now would be the best time if the test has stimulated some kind of memory recall." He then takes Dek into the adjoining room, which contains a medical bed and some high-tech equipment. "Please lie down on the bed, Decklan. Stacy, worry about those X-rays later! I need your help to set up the brain scan."

Stacy jogs over. "Just finished," she says, washing her hands in the wall sink. "Better luck this time. They're overnighting the X-rays from May 5th, 2010. You were right about the date, Decklan, and Shannon's impressed that you remembered her," she adds, getting right to work, helping Strong set up the scanning device.

"This won't hurt a bit," Strong says, attaching small electrodes around Dek's head. "This isn't anywhere near as in-depth as a CAT scan but should give us an idea about what's going on in that head of yours."

"I'm ready, just let me know what you need me to do," Dek says, slightly frightened by Strong's mad-scientist excitement.

"I want to start by getting a baseline reading, and then we'll go from there," Strong says, adjusting the knobs on the machine. "Okay, here we go! Decklan, I want you to clear your mind. Try to relax and focus on thinking one word over and over. We don't want you thinking about anything but that one word."

Dek relaxes and repeats the word *one* over and over, clearing his mind of all the memories vividly flashing back to him. A calm comes over him as he tightens his focus.

"Good," Strong whispers, like a magician trying to hypnotize an audience member. "I think that I have a solid baseline reading. Now, I want you to bring up a childhood memory, maybe of a class or vacation you took when you were very young. Try to think back as far as you can go. Make the memory as vivid and focused as you can. Good, good, Decklan," he coos as the computer screen analyzes the data coming from Dek's brain.

Dek thinks back to a memory of fishing with his dad on the dock at their family's lake house when Dek was four years old. He pictures every detail, from the feel of the worm trying to avoid being put on the hook to the tug of the line when a fish was caught. The smell of the fresh air and the feel of the warm breeze coming off the lake. The sound of a bee buzzing among the flowers lining the shore. Dek's dad fighting to get his camera out of his pocket to take a proud picture of the fish they just caught. The memory is so vivid, Dek is almost brought to tears, thinking back on such a happy time in his life.

Strong brings Dek back with a clap of his hands. "Decklan, are you still with me?" he asks.

"Yeah," Dek says groggily. "Almost fell asleep though."

"Good, that's exactly what we want," Strong assures him. "Now, I want you to concentrate on a more recent memory. Something that's happened in the past two weeks."

That's easy, Dek thinks as he recalls the moment of the accident. In this state of relaxation, it's as if he's an objective third party watching himself walk into the lab building and see the back of Lauren's head as she argues with Janet at the front desk. Then his past self gets upset with Dick for using the lab, stopping Dek from doing his work. Oh, yeah ... Dick was the one who suggested he use Dr. Martin's lab. Was he trying to get Dek in trouble? The memory continues as Dek enters Dr. Martin's lab with the key he still had from when he dated her assistant the year before. When he once again sees the tampons in the medicine cabinet, he realizes they must have been Lauren's. Then he looks at the hood and notices some dust from previous use but nothing alarming, no metal fragments. Everything looks just fine like it did before.

As he starts to do his work on the samples, a beam of light shines on the hood's surface. This must have been when Lauren came in and found him using her equipment without authorization.

The beam of light is probably from when she opened the blinds on the wall since the window was next to the hood.

Then everything slows down as if Dek is watching a movie in slow motion.

Paying careful attention to each movement in the memory, he now notices a slight smoke rising off the surface of the hood where the dust from Lauren's samples still sits. It's visible with the sunlight shining directly on it. He breathes in some of the smoke before Lauren's yelling causes him to stand up.

Wow. The vividness of the memory brings him face-to-face with the beauty and anger on Lauren's face as they meet for the first time. She's only a foot away from him, fire blazing in her gorgeous eyes.

He looks past her toward the still-open medicine cabinet on the wall. The mirror on it is redirecting the sunlight from the open window to the hood's surface. Dek tries to say something, but whatever he inhaled from the smoke is affecting him, preventing him from doing so. When he tries to speak, though, a puff of the smoke goes right into Lauren's face. Then he hears the hood alarm detecting the smoke, and a burst of red blood explodes from his hand across Lauren's face.

"Decklan, are you okay?"

Dek suddenly opens his eyes as Strong and Stacy shake him awake and yell in his ears, begging him to snap out of it. They immediately stop when they see he's conscious again and help him up into a sitting position. Stacy removes the anodes from his head as Strong puts an arm around Dek and sits next to him on the side of the bed.

"Son, are you feeling all right?" Strong asks again, calmly this time.

"I think so," Dek says, a bit disoriented, like he's just been roused from a deep sleep. "What happened?"

"The machine started to show readings indicative of you starting to have a seizure. You were moving involuntarily. We were afraid it was too much," Strong explains. "What in the world were you trying to remember?"

"The accident. It was as if I was watching it happen all over again. The memory was so vivid and real, and I noticed things I hadn't before. I think it was something Lauren was testing that caused the accident." He recites his memory to Strong, about the sunlight and the smoke he and Lauren inhaled. Everything.

Strong is silent as he thinks through what Decklan has just revealed. "I was hoping that you would choose that memory to explore as we were stimulating this photographic side of your memory through meditation. It should help us to determine what's happened to you."

Before he can continue, Lauren bursts into the other lab room, followed by Bobby and Richard. When she sees Dek and Dr. Strong in the next room, she runs over and slams her hands on the glass separating the two parts of the lab, causing it to shake a little. "The sun! It's the sun!"

CHAPTER 15

O nce Lauren calms down, the group gathers the data they collected from the day's work and prepares to go to a private meeting room to discuss the findings. Dr. Strong tells them to hold off on discussing the details of Lauren's sun theory with Bobby or Stacy for now. There's a room down the hall with a large oak conference table and a computer connected to an LED-screen display system Strong can use to present work findings. He leads everyone to the room, then briefly speaks with Bobby and Stacy, telling them to go home for the night. He finally convinces them to leave, saying they were working on a top-secret health supplement formula for a large company, and they may face legal ramifications if they reveal any of the testing results. Dek doesn't think they bought it but hopes the thought of legal action will keep them from telling anyone about the findings. Although health supplement testing sounds like a bit of a stretch for what they did today during the testing. A secret government super-soldier project might've been more believable.

After grabbing a quick bite and drink from a vending machine, the group—now just Strong, Richard, Lauren, and Dek—gather inside the conference room, with multiple file folders and Dek's X-rays.

Strong sits at the head of the table and begins the conversation. "Well, it's been a very eye-opening day for all of us. After talking with Bobby ... Lauren, it sounds like you got equally impressive results with the physical side of the testing as we did with the mental and physiological side of the testing. It will be interesting to see how things change when you switch tasks tomorrow. I know that we're all excited to share our experiences and inferences from today, but let's start at the beginning and go over everything to keep our scientific integrity intact."

They go over the notes Bobby took during Lauren's physical tests. Dek knew some fantastic things were going on with their bodies, but seeing it on paper is astounding. Lauren outperformed most gold-winning Olympic athletes. She was also able to get incredible control of her muscles and reflexes. If she needed to jump higher, her body and cells would adjust to make that happen. The results were incredible but still within the range of what could be attained by a human, not quite Superman's level. As Lauren's tests continued, her results diminished; her later tests were not as strong as when she first started. This causes them to segue into her sun theory.

Lauren tells them about how the longer she was in the dark, practically windowless gym, the more she felt her strength waning, and the minute she got outside in the sun, she was reenergized back to the way she felt at the beginning. "I've been going over everything we've experienced since the accident. I believe there's a direct correlation between the times we've lost consciousness or the times we've exceeded our normal abilities and direct contact with our skin and sunlight," she explains, determined she's on to something.

"I admit I also feel empowered when out in the sunlight, but it's summer. Anytime you're outside, your skin's in direct contact with sunlight. It seems like too much of a stretch. What about our improved vision in the pitch-black storage room? There was no sunlight there," Dek argues, trying to give some differing examples.

"I still feel that the sun must be connected in some way to what's going on in our bodies," Lauren replies with a slight shake of her head.

Dek ponders for a moment, then tells her about the smoke and sunlight he noted when he recalled the details of the accident during his brain scan test. "I'm not sure if the sunlight caused the smoke, though, or if the smoke was already there, and the sunlight illuminated it, but we definitely breathed it in. This smoke or mist or whatever it was could somehow be related to our changing bodies."

"Do you think it could've come from the samples you were working with, or do you think it was left over from the test Lauren did before you got there?" Strong asks.

"I'm not sure, but I don't think my samples were near the area the smoke was coming from," Dek says.

"Are you still trying to blame me for the accident?" Lauren exclaims.

"No! Jesus, Lauren, how many times do we have to argue about this?" Dek says, frustrated by how upset she gets when they revisit the topic of how the accident occurred. "You want me to say it? Fine, *I'm* to blame for the accident. I shouldn't have been in your lab without authorization. I completely disregarded regulations and the proper hood-cleaning protocols. The blame is all *mine*. There, you happy?"

She gives him a sad, guilt-ridden look and sighs, saying, "You're right, I'm sorry. I didn't mean to be so defensive, and I should've properly cleaned my station before I left the room. The dust or smoke could've come from my work."

After a moment of awkward silence, Dek glances at her and slowly asks, "Anyway ... what exactly were you testing?"

"So much has happened in the last few days, I guess I can tell you as much as I can without breaking my contract. Then we can decide if I need to go into more detail."

The three men hold their breath, excited to finally learn what the big secret is. Richard, in particular, seems especially nervous as Lauren starts to go over the specifics of her project.

"I was basically isolating a type of metal with a very specific radiation signature. I was told it would be used to treat and identify cancer cells, but I suspect they may have had some additional uses in mind. The samples I was working with were core drill samples, meaning they were extracted from the earth by a deep drill tower. The tower sends a drill down into the ground and extracts a sample from a specific depth and brings the sample up. In one location, they can extract many samples from various depths to figure out if what they're looking for is there and at what depth they'll need to dig to mine the material. This cuts down on companies doing huge, expensive exploratory digs to find out that they're digging in the wrong place. The samples are relatively small, about the size of a cigar tube. I basically remove the metal pieces with the radiation signature, clean the samples, and test them for the strength and type of radiation. Then I send the samples and my findings off to my contractor and get paid."

"Why would a company want you to do these tests privately instead of having it done at their own facility by their own team?" Dek asks, not realizing he's echoing Bobby's question from earlier.

"The company may not want to file their findings with any type of regulatory board. That would be a requirement if they were doing official tests," Strong interjects. "It may be that they don't want other companies to know what they have in the works, or they may have other possible uses in mind for the substance as Lauren said."

"Are we thinking this substance could've left some radiation residue on the hood, and that's what's causing the changes in us?" Dek says, beginning to piece it all together. "Lauren, did you leave any fragments of metal containing the radioactive signature on the hood's surface?"

"No," Lauren and Richard say simultaneously, causing Dek to raise an eyebrow at them.

"I mean, I highly doubt you guys have some sort of radiation poisoning," Richard backpedals. "You haven't shown any signs of sickness."

"And I took every precaution in isolating the part of my samples that could've contained any radiation. I also extensively checked over the surface area for signs of it. The only thing left on the hood's surface would've been some dust or dirt I cleaned off the samples, but the dirt contained no radioactive signature," Lauren explains.

"The morning of the accident, I saw you in the lobby, arguing with the girl at the front desk about something. What was that about?" Dek asks, wondering if there may be a connection.

"Well, let's see," Lauren says, thinking back. "I'd just mailed off my findings and was going back up to the lab to do a final clean up, organize my personal stuff, and then leave. I needed some towels and cleaner to clean up the dust and dirt I'd removed from the metal. Most of the byproduct from what I was testing was sent off in a sealed hazardous-waste container with the samples, except for some dust on the hood's area, but I'd already tested the area, and it was all free of radiation. I swear, there were no pieces of the metal remaining. I was *very* thorough."

"I believe you. I also don't remember seeing any metal fragments left on the hood," Dek reassures her. He then turns to Strong. "Do you think that the dust and dirt from the samples could've contained any chemicals or biohazard products?"

"Hard to say," Strong replies with a shrug. "It could be that the radiation from the metal was somehow keeping the biohazard in check, and by removing the radiation, you inadvertently caused it to be released."

"That doesn't make any sense!" Richard bursts in. "If that was the case, then it would've got to Lauren as soon as she removed the radiation source, or Dek when he first started working on his samples. It wouldn't have waited for Lauren to come back to affect them."

"He's right," Dek reluctantly agrees. "It doesn't add up."

"I'm still not sure what caused all of this," Strong says, perplexed. "Maybe the answer will be in the filter you recovered from the hood. There's another concern for us based on the tests we've done today."

Suddenly, Richard's phone starts to vibrate in his pocket, interrupting their conversation. After glancing down at the screen to see who it is, Richard excuses himself, leaving the room while mumbling, "Sorry, guys, I need to take this."

"This is the craziest, most interesting conversation I've had in years. Who could possibly be calling to pull you out of this room?" Strong quips, shaking his head as Richard exits into the hallway, ignoring him. "I'm actually glad that Richard's left. What I have to discuss with you two could be personal."

Lauren and Dek share a look as Strong continues. "As I was saying, the X-rays of Decklan's hand have given me cause for concern. The bone cells seem to be denser on the X-ray than what we got from the previous X-rays of Decklan's bones. This is sometimes found in types of bone cancer. I can, in no way, be sure at this point, but ..."—he hesitates for a moment before finishing his thought—"what's happening to you two could be the start of some new kind of fatal cancer."

The couple are silent as what Strong's revealed sinks in.

"But ... but that can't be. We feel great," Lauren says with a hint of desperation. "We can't be dying."

"Hold on," Strong cautions. "I didn't say it was definite. I just said it *looks* like cancer, and we have to be prepared for anything when dealing with a situation that's taking us into uncharted territory."

Giving Lauren's hand a gentle squeeze, Dek whispers, "You can't tell me it didn't cross your mind."

"No, I guess not," she replies sadly, her stomach tightening. "It just hurts to hear it out in the open from a professional."

"You know," Strong says. "I also did some skin sample tests of the hand that are equally interesting and different from what I would expect with bone cancer. Decklan's body has responded to a severe amputation by converting the cells around the injury into stem cells, the very ones that were used to create the hand when he was just a fetus. The cells then went on to recreate the part of the hand that was removed in the injury. In theory, I believe our DNA holds the starting formula to remake broken-off body parts, and, somehow, whatever you two encountered has allowed you to access and stimulate that part of your DNA."

"I guess each person's individual DNA contains the map that was originally used to create that unique person," Lauren says. "If we could call on that part of our DNA to recreate any amputations or injuries that have occurred, the ramifications of this could change the lives of millions, from soldiers to accident victims."

"Something like this could also have a very high price tag if it were marketed instead of given to the people," Strong comments, thickly laying on the harsh reality they may be dealing with. "Let's not forget the world we live in. The type of value we're talking about would demand a high level of secrecy."

They're all startled when Richard barges back into the room. "Sorry about that, guys. What did I miss?"

CHAPTER 16

After filling Richard in, the group decides it's probably a good time to call it a night. It's been a long day, and they all need some rest and time to digest what they've surmised. Cancer, stem cells, and biohazard radiation is a lot to process in one afternoon.

"I need a shower," Lauren announces as the trio returns to their hotel room. "You boys didn't go through an NFL training camp like I did today. I think my improved sense of smell is allowing me to better understand just how much I stink." She then sets down her things, goes into the bathroom, and turns on the water to shower.

Richard plops down on the couch while Dek sinks into a nearby chair, both glad to finally take a load off. They glance over at Lauren's phone on the counter when it starts to vibrate, letting her know a text message has come through. "It can wait until she's out of the shower," Dek says just as Richard gets up and peeks at her phone. "Dude, that's not cool!"

Richard picks up the phone and returns to the sofa with it. "Look, man, what do we really know about her? Seriously, what if she's working with that company now, and this is some sort of experiment they're doing on you to see if some crazy substance is going to heal you or kill you with cancer?"

Dek gives him a disapproving look and takes the phone from him. "Leave her stuff alone."

"Okay," Richard says, holding his hands up in surrender. "It was just some text from her boyfriend anyway. But I still think we have to be careful."

The air immediately leaves Dek's lungs as he mindlessly puts her phone back on the counter and returns to his seat, like someone just punched him in the gut. It never even occurred to him that she could have a boyfriend. It's not like she's done anything to squash his steadily growing feelings for her over the course of the trip. Of course such a wonderful girl would already be in a relationship, but he can't stop himself from feeling hurt and betrayed.

"Are you all right, man?" Richard asks, sensing a change in Dek's mood. "I told you; it was nothing."

"Yeah, I'm good," Dek says as they hear the shower turn off. "It's just been a long day, that's all. I'm going down to the pool for a bit." He's eager to leave the room before Lauren comes back, feeling embarrassed and not wanting to see her right now. He should've known a beautiful, intelligent, amazing girl like Lauren would have a boyfriend. *I'm so stupid*, he thinks.

Thankfully, the pool is empty, so Dek can sulk in peace. He puts his feet in the lukewarm water and stares blankly at the ripples.

After about fifteen minutes, Lauren finds him. "Hey, Richard said you were down here. Can I join you?"

"Sure," he says with a droll voice.

She sits beside him, wearing a white hotel robe, her freshly dried hair cascading around her face. Her face is fresh and makeup free, and she gives him a killer smile as she puts her hand on his. "Long day, huh?" she says sweetly, trying to draw his attention away from the water.

"Yeah," he replies coldly. "I'm dead tired." He's getting the impression she's looking for more than a friend tonight, but he's so upset about the boyfriend thing, he can't get out of his own way. "Your phone went off while you were in the shower."

"Yeah, it was just some text, though I'm not sure who it was even from."

"Really? You're sure it wasn't your *boyfriend*?" he blurts out, hurt she would try to lie about it.

"Boyfriend?" she asks, recoiling. "I never said I had a boyfriend."

"You never said you didn't either," he spits. "You don't have to lie. I know the text was from your boyfriend."

"You were going through my phone?" she yells, quickly getting to her feet. "You need to mind your own business and stay away from my stuff!" As she storms out of the pool room, she turns around and adds, "You are such a *jerk*!"

***

Lauren collapses on her bed, frustrated and angry. "Just when I think it's okay to open my heart up to someone again, he has to go and act like *such* an asshole," she whispers under her breath, knowing Richard will hear her if she talks too loudly despite being asleep on the couch.

During her final semester of college, she fell for one of her teachers who was ten years older than her. At that time, she thought he was so wise and in control of his life. She couldn't help but be attracted to him. Then she graduated and looked for opportunities to work in various labs across the country, and it drove him insane. He wanted her to become his wife and raise his kids as if she'd gone to college for six years and gotten her master's degree so she could sit around the house and babysit. One night they had a major fight about her "duties" as his girlfriend, and he ended up slapping her across the face and calling her a "selfish bitch." It was like he'd become a different person. She immediately broke up with him, her trust destroyed. No matter how many times he apologized and swore it would never happen again, she refused to take him back.

Instead, she put all her time and energy into her job at a lab for a large chemical manufacturer. Within a year, she was promoted to lab supervisor. The money was good, though her drive for success was constantly leaving her wanting more. However, she refused to fill the void with a man. She wasn't interested in any kind of romantic relationship anymore and spurned the many romantic advances from her male colleagues.

While reviewing some research the company was doing on a new skincare product, she came across a large payment made to an individual scientist who wasn't on their direct team. After doing a little digging, she learned they had paid a private contractor to secretly test this product before they began official testing to increase their chances of success and eliminate any hang-ups during the product approval process. This scientist was paid a lot of money to perform some tests that would've probably been deemed unethical or violated government lab testing policies. Lauren saw this type of work as a way to quickly make a large amount of money and free herself from strict corporate oversight.

Now her new career is in major jeopardy, and she could be dying from some new kind of cancer, not to mention a broken heart.

***

"Shit, shit, shit!" Dek hisses to himself, standing in front of their hotel room door and smacking his hand against his forehead. Of course, Lauren thinks *he's* the jerk, even though *he's* not the one who went through her phone. Fucking awesome.

He gets the courage to go inside and is relieved to see Richard passed out on the couch and Lauren asleep in her bed. The room is silent, except for a soft buzzing sound. It seems to be coming from the lamp on the work desk. He reaches in and tightens the bulb, thinking it was loose and causing the noise. When the buzzing continues, he reaches down and pulls the lamp's cord from the wall. But the noise is still there.

"What're you doing?" Richard asks groggily, waking up from the couch.

"Can you hear that buzzing sound?" Dek asks. "I think it's coming from this lamp."

"Just go to sleep, man," Richard moans, falling back down on the couch. "I'm sure the lamp isn't going to explode or anything."

Determined to find the source, Dek reaches into the shade and feels around the edge. There's a pea-sized lump near the back. He pulls it off and sees it's a small, black disk no bigger than the end of a pencil. The buzzing is definitely coming from it. He squeezes the disk between his fingers until the sound stops. "Guys, I think we need to change rooms."

Richard sits up again. "What?"

Lauren sits up, too, turning on the light on the bedside table. "What's going on?" she asks before spotting the small disk in Dek's hand.

Holding it up between his fingers, he says, "I just found a big *bug* in our room. I think it's time to go."

***

Janitor Vince is walking down the dimly lit corridor, pushing his cleaning cart and whistling, like he doesn't have a care in the world. He's wearing headphones, but there's no music playing. He halts in the middle of the hall, putting a finger up to one of his headphones. He listens carefully to the rustling sound of someone touching the speaker before all noise is abruptly cut off.

Mr. Vincent gives a sly smile, realizing someone just figured out he was listening in on them. How they found one of the bugs he left in their room, he doesn't know, but it means they'll probably find the bugs he just placed around the lab as well. It may be time to speed up his plans and end this game of cat and mouse. He reaches down into his coat pocket and taps his phone twice, and his earbuds come to life with the Rolling Stones' "You Can't Always Get What You Want." He continues pushing his cart down the hall toward the exit, dancing along to the music.

CHAPTER 17

The trio pile into Richard's car at 8 a.m., still feeling worn out and confused after finding two more bugs in their room. They spent most of the night moving their things to a new room and worrying about who could be listening to them and why. Who even knows they're there?

Dek's only solace is that all the drama momentarily took the focus off the fact he and Richard had looked at the text message on Lauren's phone. The intensity of the past few days makes him feel like they're a married couple instead of two people who just met and know nothing about each other. They need calmer heads to figure this out. There'll be time for romance and relationships later. At least, he hopes there will be.

They arrive at the lab and immediately launch into science mode. Dr. Strong, Bobby, and Stacy are already inside, having been at it for a while, preparing the lab for some new tests.

This time, Dek will go with Bobby for athletic testing, and Lauren will stay at the lab to be poked and prodded. They're both a little leery about being separated since they don't know who they can trust. What if Dr. Strong is keeping tabs on them away from the facility? Who else knows they're here or where they're staying?

After saying a stressed good-bye to Lauren, Dek and Bobby head to the gym with Richard tagging along to help compare the results.

"I don't know what you two are taking," Bobby says jokingly, "but if your results are anywhere close to Superwoman's, I'll be needing to invest some money in the nutritional company you're testing for."

Dek gives Bobby a wry smile. "If it doesn't kill us first, someone could stand to make a load of money," he says, wondering again about who's spying on them. The results they're getting are amazing. If they're just a couple of blind test subjects, and this is all some kind of setup, he's totally going to sue.

Richard leans forward, poking his head between the two, "You know, Dek, if these results can be replicated, and we can find a way to produce a product that can do for everyone what it's doing for you and Lauren, there could be a lot of money to be made."

Dek glares back at Richard. "Before we get into money, let's first try to figure out the extent of what this does and the safety aspects that could be related to taking this product."

Seeing Dek is clearly distracted, Bobby asks, "Are you guys feeling okay today? You and Lauren both seem very out of it, not as excited as you were before."

"We had a rough night," Dek answers, trying to remain vague and still explain the change in their mood. "I think we're both worried there may be large side effects associated with these supplements, and we're not sure if we're prepared to deal with them."

When they arrive at the gym, they decide to change it up a little. They move as many of the tests as they can to an outside venue. It's a partly cloudy day, but Dek can feel the sun peeking through the clouds and filling his body with power. After he runs through the same tests Lauren did both inside and outside the gym and receives similarly remarkable results, they find there's some difference between outside and inside, but it's not very significant.

"Another record-breaking performance!" Bobby exclaims. "I'm not sure what you guys are on, but I can't imagine it's legal. Is it injected or some kind of pill?"

"I think you could say it was inhaled," Dek says, trying to cool down and catch his breath.

"'Inhaled'?" Bobby questions, amazed.

"And very experimental and secret," Richard adds, letting Dek know to limit what he says.

"You're right," Dek says. "We really can't talk about it, Bobby, but keep an eye out for a new inhaled product when it hits the shelf. That is, if I don't croak."

"Well based on our data from today and your vitals after such a great workout, you could live forever," Bobby says, still excited as he looks over the test results.

"Or die of cancer tomorrow," Dek mutters sarcastically, glancing at Richard.

"Let's head back and see how Lauren's doing," Richard suggests, packing up the testing equipment. He's a little unnerved by Dek's constant focus on the negative possibilities of what's happened and not the incredible changes they're witnessing before their eyes. "You know, man—" he starts before Dek shushes him.

When Richard gives him an annoyed look, Dek points to a man standing under a tree fifty yards away and aiming a camera at them. The man quickly runs off when he realizes he's been seen. "Hey, stop!" Dek shouts, instinctively chasing after him. He's able to cross the distance in just a few seconds only to see the guy has already made it to the parking lot, tearing off in a black car. "What the hell?"

"What happened?" Bobby and Richard both ask as they reach him, panting for breath.

"I don't get it," Dek says, dumbfounded. "I thought I made it here in record time, but the guy was already in his car and driving off a block away."

"What guy?" Richard asks.

"You *did* make record time," Bobby says, finally catching his breath. "I'll bet you beat your best-timed run. Were you chasing someone?"

Dek wipes the sweat off his forehead, not sure what just happened. "I swear, I saw someone under this tree, taking pictures of us. I tore over here, but the guy was already driving off. If I made it here so fast, how did he get so far away? Was he actually *faster* than me, or am I just losing my mind, and there was no man taking pictures?"

"I'm not sure. I didn't see anyone," Richard says, patting him on the shoulder. "I think you're just stressed, man. Let's go back, as you suggested, and see what they have at the lab."

As they start walking back, Dek keeps glancing toward the tree and wondering if he really did imagine the whole thing. Could hallucinations be part of what's happening to him? God, he really hoped losing his mind wasn't another side effect. That'd just be the icing on the cake.

CHAPTER 18

Back at the lab, the testing continues at a fevered pace. Stacy already has three vials of blood for testing. Dr. Strong's examining some skin samples under the compound microscope, and Lauren's busy on the cognitive learning program, trying to beat Dek's score.

Strong steps back from the microscope and stretches his stiff back before slumping down in his comfy, oversized desk chair. He can feel the buzz of discovery in the air. It's been a long time since the lab was alive like this. It's as though he's a young man again, enjoying the early stages of a relationship, anticipating each new touch, feeling, and encounter. He glances up at a picture on the wall of his twenty-something-year-old self with a team of biotech students. He pauses, thinking back to the last big discovery moment that occurred in this lab, also involving a virus, in early 1995. He'd had a student who was working on a way to attack the HIV virus by attaching pieces of RNA to micro fragments of gold. The gold would be injected or air-blasted into the virus-containing cell in an attempt to stop viral replication.

After a few weeks of testing and some very promising results, they were cleared to do human experimentation. The process was fast-tracked due to the fear and misunderstanding that was circulating the country about the virus. The lack of real public understanding of how the virus was transmitted, or the extent the virus could kill the infected person, made many people worry about a pandemic. Strong was new to the research side of his position at the university and eager to make a big discovery. He knew they had good initial findings, but he also had serious reservations about the full effectiveness of the treatment inside an infected patient. Ignoring his gut, he agreed to run the tests on ten late-stage HIV patients. Unfortunately, the RNA failed to correctly incorporate itself with the active virus, and two of the patients died from AIDS during the trials. At the same time, other oral antiviral treatments were coming out that could have potentially allowed these patients to live. Multiple students on Strong's team were crushed by the failure and losses of life. Some even gave up on pursuing careers as scientific researchers. For Strong, it was mentally stunning.

Ever since then, he's spent most of his academic years focusing on refining others' ideas rather than branching out for new discoveries. He's become overly cautious, afraid to make another big mistake. Whenever a risky or scary piece of new research comes into his office, he looks at the picture of his old team as a deterrent, to remind himself of the risks and give him the strength to reject many interesting projects. Now, looking at the smiling faces and visible excitement in himself and his team, along with the excitement Decklan and Lauren have brought into his life, he's starting to remember the joy and excitement of a new scientific discovery.

After about twenty-five minutes, Lauren pushes away from the computer screen, raising her hands triumphantly. "Done!" Glancing back at Strong, she eagerly asks, "How'd I do? Did I beat Dek's time and score?"

Strong gets up from his chair, taking one last glance back at the picture before walking over. "You beat his time, but I don't think he was racing."

As he types in some codes, Lauren fidgets in her seat, barely able to contain her excitement. "Dek was right. This is the first time I've tried to really focus on the cognitive side of my powers—or reaction or side effects or whatever you call it. I can't believe the memory recall and speed that my thoughts are processing at. If this had happened to me during school, I'd have fifty degrees and speak twenty languages."

Strong straightens up. "I'm afraid Dek beat you."

"What? That can't be right," Lauren blurts out.

"Yep, he got you by one answer," Strong states, nodding his head.

"Well then I want a rematch!" Lauren whines, leaning back in her chair. "So what's next?"

Strong has Lauren follow him over to where he's testing some skin cells he took after scraping Lauren's arm and some cells from a swab of her mouth. "Your cells are five times more reactive to stimulus than a normal human cell," he explains. "This indicates that your cells are capable of receiving many more signals than normal ones. This, in some ways, helps us to understand how you're able to almost mentally call on your individual muscle cells to make you stronger or increase your endurance during physical exertion. This may also help us understand how the neurons in your brain are firing faster and increasing your ability to remember and recall information accurately. These cells aren't just more reactive to stimulus, they're also intuitive. You could call them 'smart cells,' making adjustments to the needs of the body on a subconscious, as well as conscious, level."

Strong pauses, allowing Lauren a chance to process the information.

"Allowing us to heighten our senses by concentrating. What could have changed us on a molecular and cellular level?" Lauren asks, staring at the computer screen's cell comparisons.

"I have some ideas for that as well," Strong says, directing her to a different computer screen. "We've received a few of your blood tests, and the results are indicative of a person who has the flu—"

"But we don't feel sick!" Lauren interrupts, still terrified by the idea of dying from some new cancer. "In fact, we feel better than ever."

"Your white blood cell counts are elevated, but in a different way than we would typically find in someone with the flu. I believe you have encountered a virus, but not a regular one. It's entered your body and is multiplying, working in conjunction with your body. Instead of your body having an immune response, causing you to have cold symptoms, it's altering your RNA to allow you to access greater portions of your DNA."

Again, Strong pauses, letting Lauren come to grips with what he's saying, as well as formulating his own thoughts about his theory.

"So what we're assuming is that we've contracted a virus from the substance in the hood, and this virus, rather than making us sick, is changing the way our body reads our DNA," Lauren summarizes, "allowing us to access abilities that were always in our DNA but inactive up until now."

"Yes," Strong confirms. "Our DNA strands are very long. It's been surmised that we only use a small portion of our DNA, and the rest could be considered junk DNA, only there to position the important parts of our DNA to be read correctly by the RNA, eliciting the responses that cause our bodies to function. What I believe we're seeing in your case is a virus changing how your body reads its DNA. Instead of junk DNA, it's simply unread DNA. The sections we've long considered to be placeholders could actually be the blueprint for our next stage of evolution. Instead of the virus causing an immune response from your body to fight off the virus, it's working *with* your body to change all your cells."

Lauren continues along Strong's thought path. "The changes we're experiencing are things that are in every human's DNA. The virus has allowed us to access these abilities, but really, anyone could."

"You may be just getting the tip of the iceberg," Strong says. "If this is a total cellular change involving senses, muscles, healing, aging, and brain function, this could change the human race as we know it. People could live longer, healthier lives with greater brain function and information retention. This could allow the great brains of our time to live on and advance our race far beyond our current existence. What if our life expectancy were two hundred years old instead of eighty? Just think of the things we could accomplish. Our brains working at a higher level could process more advanced thoughts." Strong's staring off, as if the gravity of what he's saying is blowing his own mind. "You're evolving right before our eyes. It's long believed that we have evolved as a species in leaps rather than the small changes of natural selection. It's possible that these leaps may be triggered by a virus."

He stops and looks over Lauren's shoulder as Dek, Richard, and Bobby enter the lab. "Hello, fellow scientists," Dek announces, walking over to where Strong and Lauren have been discussing their theories, and taking a seat next to Lauren. "What's up?"

"We may be solving the mysteries of human evolution," Lauren simply states, as if they were talking about the weather.

CHAPTER 19

The team breaks for lunch, allowing for a crumb-filled debate as the others are brought up to speed on what's going on. After conferring with Dr. Strong, Lauren and Dek decide the potential ramifications of what they're experiencing are too great not to share with the entire team, so they include Bobby and Stacy in their discussion.

The looks of shock are abundant as Dek looks from face to face around the conference table. Bobby, Richard, and Dek go over the results from Dek's athletic testing, and Strong shares with them what he's observed with Lauren's tests. The basic premise of their hypothesis is they're the first evolved people of a potentially new form of the human race. The idea is absolutely crazy but seems to fit with the evidence they've gathered so far.

"The virus is in our blood," Dek says. "Can it be transferred to others, just like a regular virus, or is it more of a blood-transferred virus, like HIV?"

Strong is the first to answer. "You first encountered the virus by inhaling it, so it can become airborne. No one you've had close contact with has shown any signs of the virus, which leads me to believe that once it's in your system, changing your DNA, it must remain blood-borne."

"If this is a step in the evolution of mankind, the virus would need to have a way to affect all the areas of the world. An airborne delivery system would be the most effective way to do this," Lauren adds.

"I'll take a sample of Decklan's blood and mix it with samples from each of us to see how normal cells react to viral-loaded blood. Maybe that will help us determine how the virus is transferred," Strong says.

"The samples Lauren was working with didn't affect her until she surprised Dek in the lab. Was something keeping the virus in check, or were the radioactive protective measures you were using in the lab stopping viral transmission?" Richard asks.

"Good question," Strong replies. "What do you think, Lauren? You had the most contact with the virus and the samples it came from."

"The samples were highly radioactive, and I had to wear protective gear at all times, but the dust that was left on the hood's surface was clear of any radioactive signature. I was around the dust without protective gear for some time after the samples were removed, and I was unaffected until the accident."

"Until the sunlight reflected off the mirror of the medicine cabinet and shined on the surface of the hood," Dek adds, remembering his earlier mental testing with Strong. "The sunlight could be the catalyst, triggering the release of the virus. I didn't notice the smoke or steam until the sunlight was reflected on the hood."

"Yes, I think you could be right," Lauren confirms. "I had the window open at other times but not with the cabinet door open. That was what directed the sunlight from the window onto the hood's surface—"

"Activating the virus," they finish in unison.

"It only took seconds in direct contact with the activated virus for us both to pass out," Dek says. "The virulence must be off the charts."

"We know how you two reacted to the virus, but I'm not so sure everyone will react in the same way," Strong cautions. "What if natural selection still has a role to play? It may be that you two had DNA compatible with the virus, but the same results may not occur for everyone. Speaking of evolution, we're not sure what happened to the dinosaurs. What if a similar virus was released, maybe by a meteor strike, causing an evolution in one type of species and, at the same time, causing the extinction of another?"

Lauren shakes her head. "You're suggesting all life on the planet makes large leaps in evolution due to a virus being released into the atmosphere that infects all or most of the life on the planet. The cells of all creatures are affected, with some making a leap forward and some getting completely killed off. What about natural selection and the gradual evolution of life?"

"It's possible that both forms of evolution are occurring. The large leaps could explain how a fish could become a land animal when natural selection would make the chance of success almost impossible. You could also have the slower evolution, like the giraffes with the longest necks reaching more leaves, causing them to be more prominent than giraffes with short necks," Strong replies.

"Let's just try some blood tests and go from there," Dek says, cautiously optimistic, his mind blown by the scope of the conversation.

***

They all return to the lab, and Stacy draws blood from everyone. The more samples they have to look at, the better idea they'll have if this could be potentially harmful. Strong then prepares his microscope apparatus and sets up the testing area. They will try a variety of tests, using whole blood and blood plasma. Lauren and Dek try to use their lab experience to help with the setup, but Strong likes to do things himself, and they quickly get the feeling they're just getting in his way.

Dek motions Lauren over to a sofa along the back wall. Again, it seems they can't find two minutes to talk to one another, and he still feels bad about looking at her phone the other night. Lauren plops down next to him on the couch. Even the slightest touching of their legs starts to send his brain into a hormone-induced fog. She has an incredible effect on him. Shaking his head slightly, he starts by saying, "How has the testing been? We haven't really been able to talk much over the last twenty-four hours."

"Good," Lauren says, adjusting in her seat but keeping a very small distance between them. "Strong says you beat my score on the intelligence test, but we were both off the charts."

"All this time, I thought you were the brains of this operation," he says jokingly before clearing his throat. "Look, I wanted to say I'm sorry for looking at your text messages the other night. It's fine that you have a boyfriend or whatever." He mutters the last part, trying poorly to hide his hurt feelings.

"Thanks for the apology. I also think I went a little overboard with the severity of the offense," she acknowledges. "It's hard to trust someone you've just met, let alone in the crazy circumstances we're going through. I can't say I wouldn't be looking at your phone if it pinged a text late at night."

"Well, I think that, more than ever, we need to be on the same team," Dek says, sounding very serious for once as he reaches for her hand. "You know, if this virus kills everyone else, we may need to repopulate the entire planet."

"At least we'll know that the new population will have lots of funny jokes," she replies with a smile, squeezing his hand. "Seriously, what do you think? Are we on the right track? This all seems so unbelievable."

"I'm not sure, but I think someone else is on to us. Not only the bugs in our room last night, but I thought I saw someone taking pictures of my outdoor testing earlier." Lauren gives him a shocked look. "I tried to run after the cameraman, but he was gone before I got there. I'm really not sure that I didn't imagine it all."

"I keep feeling like we're being watched or followed, but I can't say I've seen anyone or have anything more than just a feeling," Lauren says.

"I just want to be as honest with you as I can be," Dek says, giving her a guilty look. "I felt like I violated your trust and didn't want that to get in the way if things start to get crazy again."

"Don't worry. I can tell you're telling the truth," she says with a sly smile.

He raises an eyebrow. "How?" he asks, thinking men will be in a world of trouble if this new evolution means women can always tell when they're lying.

"You can probably do it too," she says, excited she's figured out something before him. "I can smell the changes in your pheromones and hear the changes in your heartbeat if you lie about something. It's really cool. Try it. Ask me a question and see if you can tell if I'm lying."

He can see from her mischievous expression that she's going to try to mask some of the responses he's trying to detect, but he takes on the challenge. "I thought I picked up something like that in my last conversation with Richard," he says.

"It's hard to tell with him," she replies. "I think he lies a lot. Ask a few easy ones first to establish a baseline."

Dek leans back, staring into her eyes. Her mouth holds a slight smile as she prepares for his question. "Were you just in a lab accident that changed your life?" he asks, starting with a true response.

"Yes," she replies.

She smells the same as usual, so he continues. "Do you own a cat named Mr. Sparkles?"

She starts to laugh. "'Mr. Sparkles?' Where on Earth did you come up with that?"

"Just answer the question, ma'am," he says in a detective voice.

"Yes," she says, still giggling.

Knowing this can't be the truth, he leans toward her, closing his eyes and sniffing to get a good whiff. He's definitely getting a change in her scent. He opens his eyes and sees they're only inches apart. Her eyes are ablaze, looking directly into his. He can feel the sexual electricity building between them. "Are you starting to fall for the brilliant young scientist that you recently were in an accident with?" he asks, causing a distinctive change in her smell and a blush on her cheeks.

"Hey, love birds," Richard says, walking over to the couch, "Strong wants your help analyzing the blood results. I think he's just about done."

"Sure thing," Dek says, leaning back and trying to break free of Lauren's hypnosis.

"Could you smell the difference?" she asks, smiling knowingly.

"I don't know what I was smelling, feeling, experiencing, but I think I'm going to need to work on honing that skill on someone else because I just can't think straight, being that close to you," he admits, standing up from the couch. They're still holding hands, and he gently pulls up. "You still haven't answered my question," he adds, not letting her get away that easily.

"I was hoping you could sense the unspoken answer. Maybe we can try some other tests later," she purrs, letting go of his hand and giving him a flirtatious wink.

"Hey, Dek, got a minute?" Richard asks as Lauren exits the room.

"Yeah, what's up?"

"I was thinking that if these tests go well, and it seems like the virus is transmissible through blood, then I would like to volunteer to be the next test subject."

"Oh, I don't know, Richard. I wouldn't do anything that might put you at risk."

"I'm a man of science," Richard practically shouts. "I'd be proud to take on any risks to further our quest for knowledge."

Dek looks at him, picking up on some of the signals he and Lauren were just discussing. "I think these may be the last tests we perform on ourselves. This is too big, and there's too much at stake to start human trials without a lot more research."

Richard looks down, clearly disappointed. "Okay, I see what you mean," he says reluctantly.

They walk into the room where Strong and Lauren are intently examining the blood slides on the multiple computer screens behind his desk. It takes Dek a minute to refocus his attention off every movement of Lauren's body. "Where are we in the process?" he asks Strong, trying to figure out how he has the screens set up.

"I've been doing a side-by-side comparison of both of your blood samples versus my blood sample and Richard's. The blood samples from both of you look very similar to ours until we add sunlight," Strong explains, showing the sunlight-exposed samples. "It's as if our samples have come alive!"

Strong and Richard's normal cells are floating in space, moving slowly through the plasma while the viral cells are almost jumping around, or maybe quivering, in anticipation.

"If we look closer at the cells, on a micro level, the cell walls seem to be more permeable, allowing for the transfer of more fluid and information between the cell and the environment," Strong continues, zooming in on one cell from Dek's sample. "This is one way of observing the cells out in the open, but I believe that, in the body, your neurons and neurotransmitters are also functioning in this highly communicative state. This allows the brain to communicate with the cells and the cells to react more specifically. If you need to see better, the brain sends the command to your optic cells so they can adjust. If you need to run faster, the brain can send the message to your skeletal system and neurons to increase muscle permeability, contractibility, and contract strength, making you consciously faster. Most great athletes are born with these adaptations, but you can *create* them."

"I see what you're saying, doc, but how's the virus doing this? Will it lead to cancer?" Dek asks, still observing the computer screens.

"I don't think it will," Strong responds kind of noncommittally. "The cells can replicate and change much more than regular cells, but they seem to maintain control. The cells in your damaged hand were able to revert to a stem cell-like form to recreate your hand from your existing DNA. But after they were finished reproducing the missing digits, they stopped replicating and reverted back to regular cells."

"I just can't believe this is possible. This virus could heal people who have lost limbs or can't hear or see. It could make us faster, smarter, and extend life expectancy!" Dek says, amazed by the possibilities.

"Not so fast, my friend," Strong says. "There's a probability that the DNA markers that allow this to be the response of the virus may not be in everyone's DNA."

Dek stops to consider, then asks, "So, you're saying this is the response Lauren and I have had to the virus, but that could be because we possess a gene that allows the virus to work, and not every human may have this gene?"

"Correct," Strong confirms, slumping back into his overstuffed chair.

"Or ..." Lauren chimes in, "could this virus act negatively inside a person who doesn't possess the correct genome?"

Strong gives her a solemn look. "Yes, if we're talking about this being some sort of viral evolution, as we've said, many times in Earth's history, the evolution of one species has accompanied the extinction of another. Don't see many short-necked giraffes, do you?"

They all pause.

"I think the next logical step is to test the viral transmission with our own blood samples in the lab setting, not within someone's body," Strong finally says, rolling up his sleeve to draw blood and glancing at his watch. "It's two o'clock now, so let's get the team together and do some tests before we lose the sunlight."

CHAPTER 20

D r. Strong calls Bobby and Stacy back into the lab to help them with the next steps. They all get additional blood drawn and set up a row of test samples. The idea is to combine Dek's and Lauren's blood with the samples from Strong, Richard, Bobby, and Stacy to see if they can get viral transmission and a good look at how their cells react to the virus. They've positioned the test materials in front of a west-facing window with the blackout curtains closed. They'll do an initial test in the dark, then allow the sunlight to fall on the samples to get a direct comparison.

"All set, doc," Dek says as he and Lauren finish setting up the last sample.

There are nine different samples set up along the table, each containing two blood samples separated by a glass divider. The samples are in glass dishes on an agitator to allow for slight agitation to assist in mixing the samples. They've decided no one should be allowed in the room since they're adding a sunlight component and don't want the virus to become airborne and infect any of them.

The first eight samples are Dek's blood with each of the four regular blood samples, then Lauren's blood with each of the four samples to see if there's any difference between the blood and reactivity with each sample. The final sample is the two viral blood samples mixed in case, for some reason, they have different strains of the virus and to see how this would react.

The team's located in a separate room with a glass window, allowing them visual access.

"Okay," Strong says. "Let's get the show on the road!"

"Hey, Dek," Richard says, leaning over one of the keyboards. "Looks like we have the same blood type. Should be a great experiment for compatibility with the virus."

Strong types something on his laptop, and the dividers lift from the dishes, allowing the samples to mix. The agitator starts to slowly move the dishes, making a more uniform mix of the samples. Everyone else stands at Strong's computer bank on the side of the room where they can see different angles of the samples and microscopically zoom in to look at the blood samples from a cellular level. "How does it look?" Strong asks, looking over Dek's shoulder.

"The samples are mixing well, but we're not seeing anything significant from a micro or macro level. We can't see any signs of viral actions," Dek answers him.

Strong pauses the agitator and comes over to the screens. "Your blood cells don't look as active as they did with the sunlight amplification earlier. We may have to move on to step two and bring on the light." He then moves back to his position at the window and begins typing in the commands to open the shades, letting in the light. Lauren accompanies him, eager to see if there's any visual change of the samples through the window. The sun's starting to go down, and the light coming in the window is very intense, causing both Lauren and Strong to squint and look away as their eyes adjust to the glare.

It's not so much what they see at this instant as what they hear. *Pop! Pop! Pop! Pop! Pop! Pop!*

Within seconds of the sunlight hitting the samples, six of the nine dishes have erupted in a mass of cells and blood. The mixtures of milliliters of blood have turned six of the samples into blobs the size of golf balls.

Strong and Lauren are staring in disbelief. "Did you get that, Decklan?" shouts Strong who's quickly typing on his laptop. He closes the blinds and commands the computer to check the air for particulate. "I'm showing the room's air is clear, and it looks like the virus didn't go airborne from the blood. And I'm shutting the blinds to hopefully stop the reaction!"

"I think I got the reaction on tape. We just need to slow it down a bit," Dek says, typing commands to rewind and slow down the film so they can see exactly what happened.

"It popped so fast, and the light was a little blinding, so I didn't see much," Richard adds over Dek's shoulder.

"Decklan, why don't you put on a hazmat suit and go in to check on the samples? Since you're already infected with the virus, I believe you'll be the least at risk of complication," Strong instructs. "Let me have a look at the recording. I'm pretty good at manipulating the images to give us the best comparison views."

Dek quickly puts on the suit, and Lauren helps him with sealing it up as Strong sets up at his computer array. "Did you see that, Dek?" she whispers. "I'm not sure what happened yet, but that can't be good."

Dek gives her a solemn nod from inside the suit and enters through the door to examine the samples. He moves slowly to the table since there's a bloody ooze driving down the front. Three of the dishes are intact and look fairly normal, but the other six are broken, and the blood cells have formed into a mass of tissue. He uses an aseptic technique to clean up the mess, careful to protect what they have left of the samples for further analysis. It takes him at least half an hour to completely clean the area and secure the samples.

Lauren comes over to help him out of his suit as he exits the room. The others are gathered around Strong and his bank of computers, and Dek can hear a hum of excited chatter coming from them. He cranes his neck to see what's going on.

"They're watching the slow-motion feeds from the experiment. It's pretty crazy," Lauren explains, seeing the questioning look on his face.

"Thanks for cleaning up, Dek," Strong says, rotating his chair toward the couple as they make their way to the computer. "Did you notice anything new that we may not have seen in here?"

Dek leans in toward the computer screens. "Six of the samples appear to have become very cancerous very quickly, forming a cell mass and breaking the dishes. I'm assuming these samples didn't contain the gene compatible with the virus and became cancerous?" He pauses as the screens show a second-by-second loop of the chemical reaction. "Three of the dishes appear to not react to the mixing, which is probably viral compatibility similar to what happened to Lauren and me." He hesitates before asking, "Is that the micro of the noncancerous samples?"

"You're on the right track," Strong confirms with a nod. "The six dishes that broke all had a similar reaction irrelevant to whether the blood was yours or Lauren's. Once the sun hit the samples, the virus spewed forth from the host cells and caused the nonviral cells to rapidly multiply into a cancerous mass. The blood oozing down the table was the blood from you two. This was obviously a very extreme situation, putting the sunlight directly on the cells rather than the cells being inside somebody. I would conclude from this initial experiment that if this virus were inside the body of a host who didn't have gene compatibility, it would result in a very virulent cancer and kill the host within a few hours, or days maybe, depending on the amount of sunlight exposure." Strong pauses to let this sink in.

Dek shakes his head slowly. "My god ... Lauren and I could've been killed by that accident. It was just dumb luck that we're both gene compatible."

"More than dumb luck," Lauren says, also looking at the slow-motion playback. "It appears that maybe one in four people will have this gene. Maybe twenty-five percent. The odds were highly against us both surviving."

"Obviously, this is just a preliminary experiment, and much greater research must be done to truly draw such a grim conclusion," Strong interjects, trying to keep things hopeful. "We also have some other results," he adds with a little smile. "It seems that Stacy also possesses the compatible genome. Your cells had a similar reaction in her samples, but the result was much different. On a macro level, the sample appears to almost quiver as the virus is released and quickly integrates with her cells. On a micro level, we can see cell wall penetration and RNA integration. We have a complete reconfiguration at the cellular level. The cells are changing and becoming closer to what we're seeing in the original infected samples procured from the two of you."

They all glance over at Stacy who gives them an odd grin and shrugs. "Who knew I'm special too?"

"That doesn't really tell us anything," Richard whines, sounding slightly jealous. "With such a small sample size and lack of true controls, this is very inconclusive. I think any of our cells could react positively, giving any of us the same results as these two. The speed and severity we've observed in the experiment may be why you both had reactions similar to passing out when you first fully encountered the sun after your initial infection."

"'Similar to passing out?' I was *out cold* after falling down those steps. I could've broken my damn neck!" Dek exclaims, giving a quick throat-slashing motion with his hand.

"I had a milder reaction," Lauren adds. "I just calmly sat down and fell asleep."

"Lucky you," Dek scoffs.

"I think this may be because Decklan directly inhaled the virus and then exhaled it in your face. You might not have gotten the full dosage of the virus like he did," Strong explains.

"Well, this is all very interesting," Stacy interrupts, glancing down at her phone. "But it's getting late, and I haven't eaten much. Is anyone else up for a refuel?"

In the excitement over the experiment, they all lost track of time, and Dek is ravished with hunger. "That's a great idea. I'm starving!" he says.

"I'll take Richard and run out for some food and refreshments. You guys can continue trying to figure out how to make me a superhuman," Stacy jokes, taking Richard's arm and heading for the door.

"It'll take one helluva super virus to make you anything more than super *lame!*" Bobby teases, earning him a glare from Stacy. "Pizza, by the way. Pizza would be great. Thanks!" he adds with a smirk as Stacy slams the door in his face.

CHAPTER 21

Richard abruptly stops and checks his phone as he and Stacy enter the hallway. "Hey, give me fifteen minutes to respond to this email I just got. Do you think it's okay to find some quiet in the sample room?"

"Sure," Stacy says with a shrug. "I think everyone's busy working on the test results. That should be a fairly private space. I have a few emails to check as well. Meet you back here in fifteen."

When she goes down the hall into a small office, Richard enters the sample room where all the blood samples drawn for the experiment are being kept. He checks the hall and room for privacy before shutting and locking the door. Then he immediately goes to the blood containment fridge and rifles through the sample vials of blood until he finds one labeled "DT" with yesterday's date on it. In one of the drawers, he finds a syringe and blood drawing equipment. He uses the syringe to draw up about 3 ccs of Dek's blood from the sample vial.

"We have the same blood type, so this should work," he says quietly to himself as he flicks the syringe, removing any air bubbles. "Once my blood is changed, containing the same viral load as Dek's, I'll be able to market and sell my own blood as a miracle cure. I'll make a small fortune and finally be out from under my benevolent stepfather's influence."

He injects the blood into the top of his right glute, hoping that, by injecting it intramuscularly, it'll slow down the viral transmission and not cause him to black out like the others did. He discards the syringe and applies a bandage to the injection site.

I don't feel any different yet, he thinks as he reenters the hallway, noticing the sun has just gone below the horizon. If their guess is correct, that should also help to slow the viral transmission. He leans against the wall to wait for Stacy, wondering what it'll be like to have so much speed and strength—and soon, wealth. How could he be expected to pass up an opportunity like this?

He pushes off the wall as Stacy emerges from the office she was using, still typing on her phone. "Wow, I can't believe the crazy discoveries and breakthroughs we're making!" he says, trying to sound nonchalant, but not realizing he's beginning the process of nervously talking Stacy's ear off. "Where are we going for food? What're we having? I think I'm okay with pizza if you are." He continues to ramble as Stacy continues checking her phone.

"There's a pizza place around the block that's not too bad. I'd also like to get a couple of bottles of champagne to celebrate our discoveries," she replies.

Richard's phone starts to buzz as they enter the lobby. "I'm sorry, I have to take this," he says to Stacy with a frown when he sees who it is. He diverts to a small vending machine room off to the side.

"Okay, Mr. Popular! I'll see if I can order the pizza ahead while you take your call," Stacy yells after him.

"Hello, Mr. Helms. I hope all is well with you," Richard answers, trying to act professional.

"Cut the crap, Richard," Helms says sternly. "Do you have the filter?" One quick question, no polite small talk.

"Uh, no, sir, I haven't been able to get my hands on it yet. I think Strong has it locked up in the lab."

"So you're saying you don't even know *where* my filter is? Well then, I'd like to hear your plan for recovering it," Helms growls, losing his patience.

"Look, sir," Richard stammers. "I know the basic area it's in. These guys are all caught up in some super-soldier, evolutionary, mega-virus theory. They're not really paying attention to anything else, so I should be able to locate it and retrieve it in the next couple of days."

"I have my doubts. The sample I had Summers testing has moved on to the next phase. We've acquired the land that was identified as having access to the metal, politicians have been bought, and equipment is being moved into place to start mining. I'm telling you this so you understand there's no room for failure or slip-ups. All ends must be tied up, nice and neat," Helms stresses.

"Yes, sir," Richard is quick to reply. "I understand. I'll get the filter tonight."

After a sigh, Helms adds, "I've sent you a containment envelope that you can put the filter in and send it to me in the mail. This envelope was made specifically to fit this filter and keep it from being detected in the mail, so don't lose it. I'll send you the address, and you must go and get it *immediately*."

"But I was just running out for something ..." Richard begins, only to stop and say, "Yes, sir, right away. I'll get the filter and have it shipped to you by tomorrow."

"That's better," Helms coos, ever the patronizing bastard. "Report to me when it's on its way. Goodbye, Richard."

"And have a shitty day to you too," Richard hisses into his phone after the call is disconnected, knowing he must quickly come up with an excuse to bail on helping Stacy with the food. He exits the room and finds Stacy still on her phone. "Any luck with the food?"

"Yep, they're cooking up the pies. They should almost be done by the time we get there," she says, ready to get going.

"Um, don't hate me, but I have to run an errand for my stepdad," Richard says apologetically. Stacy's been nice to him, so he hates to think he's letting her down. "He found out I was down here and needs something picked up right away. I'm really sorry about this. Is it okay if I catch up with you after dinner?"

"Sure, no problem! I can handle the food and drinks," she says, pulling out her keys. "Just don't take too long, or you'll miss all the fun."

"Thanks for understanding," Richard says as they exit the building and go their separate ways. "Save me a glass of wine!"

"Will do!" Stacy yells over her shoulder, pulling out her phone as she continues around the corner toward the pizza shop.

CHAPTER 22

Back at the lab, Bobby's trying to clean up the lab research area, checking to make sure they removed any of the blood samples or possible infective materials. Strong, Dek, and Lauren are back at Strong's desk, still somberly watching the experiment clips and collecting their thoughts.

"This is a slightly morbid question," Lauren begins, breaking the silence, "but would the world be better off if Dek and I had died in that accident? I mean, it's like we're the modern-day Typhoid Mary. The patient zero of an apocalyptical virus, ending human life as we know it." She stops to take a shaky breath.

"You may be correct," Strong says, maybe being a little too logical and honest. "But the fact is that you *are* alive, and we need to process what's happening to hopefully prevent that very thing from occurring. I know you both have some things hanging over you that are making you reluctant to go public with the situation, but given the possible significance of what we've found out thus far and possible risk to Earth's population, I think it's time to seek out help." He looks at the couple for validation that they're on board with his decision.

They look at each other and nod. "If this is as serious as we've seen in our last experiment, we can't risk this getting out. If this virus goes airborne, it could affect millions of people," Dek says, frightened by the thought of possibly causing so many deaths.

"We also need to consider the company that had Lauren running the samples. They may have more samples or a significant amount of the metal, and the virus is just waiting for light exposure to bring it to life," Strong says before focusing on Lauren. "You'll have to break your confidentiality agreement for the benefit of the public. We're assuming it's the radioactive metal they're interested in and not the virus, but they could inadvertently release the virus in the discarded material after mining and refining the metal."

"I knew it wouldn't be a secret I could keep as soon as all this craziness with Dek and me started," Lauren admits. "I just hope we'll make it in time. I think they were awaiting my results before they started a full mining project, but companies like these are run by very forward thinkers and may already be moving." She slides to one of the computer screens. "I was contacted by a private third-party entity to further keep the experiments confidential. As I worked, I reported to a ghost email set up for me so I could contact them without knowing who the information was going to. I think it was being routed through many servers before it was accessed by the final user."

"How do you know that?" Dek asks. "Were you already trying to figure this out?"

"When you were hurt and in the hospital, I was working on covering my ass, thinking the injury would bring my work out in the open." Lauren pauses, thinking a moment before continuing. "Wait, why *wasn't* all my work brought out in the open?" she asks aloud with a slight tilt of her head. "A lab accident like that would involve an extensive investigation. Am I wrong, or has the whole thing just been swept under the carpet?"

"I think that's exactly what happened," Strong interjects, typing on his middle keypad. "When we asked for Decklan's X-rays from the accident and found that the records were missing from the hospital, I looked into finding out more about the accident in the media reports and only found a report of a lab fire in the building you were working in. That happened the day you came here. I'm assuming this was to cover some tracks, especially since there's little to no mention of your accident."

"A fire in the same building our accident occurred in? That's insane! Lauren, we need to figure out who you were working for, and soon, before they accidentally release the virus," Dek says, now feeling the overwhelming gravity of the situation.

"In case you haven't noticed, Dek," Lauren says, "I think they're already trying to tie up two loose ends—you and me. The bugs in our room, the weird guy taking photos of you training, the crazy janitor locking us in the lower storage room at the lab? They've probably been on to us from the very beginning."

Dek leans back in his chair with his hands on his head. "What if they're trying to kill us to stop the spread of the virus? What if they're just greedy and don't care who they hurt to make money? God, either way, we are *fucked*!"

"I didn't know about all these incidents," Strong says. "We may need to take you to authorities tomorrow for your own protection."

They nearly jump out of their skin when Stacy kicks the door open, balancing three large pizza boxes while holding a brown paper bag under her arm. "Hey, folks, food's here! I also grabbed some bubbly so we can celebrate. I hope you're hungry," she says from the doorway.

Dek rushes over to grab the pizza boxes and helps her into the room. "Smells great," he says, glad to have a break from the earlier conversation. Things were getting way too heavy for his liking.

Strong pulls out some paper plates, and Bobby comes back from his cleanup duties. Stacy pops the cork off a bottle of champagne and fills up five plastic cups as the others fill their plates and bellies.

"Where's Richard?" Dek slurs, his mouth half-full of food.

"He had to run an errand for his stepdad. He said it was very urgent," Stacy replies, also quickly diving into the food. "So what did I miss? When do I get my superpowers?"

"I think we're going to have to get more help. This just seems like it will be too big for us to handle alone," Lauren says. "Maybe the police? Or the CDC or someone else?"

"Wow, big step," Stacy says, wiping pizza sauce off her chin. "Did you guys think of the religious ramifications of your new evolution?"

Lauren and Dek exchange a glance. Being science majors, they'd only been focused on that side of the evolutionary argument.

"You two could be defined as the next coming or be prosecuted for saying what's happening to you is a form of evolution. You're not supporting natural selection, but you're definitely contradicting creation," Stacy adds.

"I think it's all in the way you look at it," Strong says, sipping some champagne. "You could just as easily say the virus is God's way of changing and progressing his people. That it's his will for the virus to be released."

"I think we may need more alcohol if we're going to go down the theological path. Isn't the scientific path enough for you people?" Dek jests, raising his glass just as his vision starts to blur and his head grows heavy. "Damn, this stuff is really strong."

When he glances around, he notices Bobby and Lauren have passed out, slumping over in their chairs. Strong's in the same condition. Dek tries to stand, but his legs aren't responding. He squints at a fully conscious Stacy before falling off his chair. *She never touched her drink*; he realizes as he passes out on the floor.

"Sweet dreams, big guy," Stacy says, grabbing a bottle of white wine from the bag and pouring herself a glass before pulling out her phone. "You're good to go."

CHAPTER 23

Dek peels open his heavy eyelids but can't move the rest of his body. He can see Stacy on her phone, sitting in a chair against the wall behind Lauren, but from this angle, he can't see Strong or Bobby. Lauren appears to be okay, though she's lying still, her face turned toward him and away from Stacy. He can tell she's breathing, but her eyes are still closed.

He can remember Stacy saying something as he passed out, but his throbbing head only recalls a muffled sound. He looks at the door when he hears footsteps coming from the hall. It also sounds as though someone's pushing a rolling cart. It's after regular hours, so Dek's not sure who it could be. *Maybe it's Richard!* he thinks, realizing he never came back after Stacy brought the food.

The door opens, and a janitor pushes a cart into the room. The same janitor the trio ran into back in Madison.

Vince.

What's he doing here?

Dek looks from the door to Lauren and sees she's also awake and still paralyzed, looking shocked and terrified. Then she closes her eyes to pretend she's still unconscious.

"Looks like you've made quite a mess," Vince says, rolling in his janitor's cart and closing the door behind him. "Perfect time for the janitor to arrive for a little cleanup."

"That stuff you gave me to put in their drinks was very effective," Stacy replies, looking proudly over her work. "They all went down without a fight."

"That one has his eyes open," Vince says, gesturing Dek's direction. "Did he not drink it all?" he asks, squatting down near Dek's face.

"I saw him finish the glass," Stacy replies sharply, getting up from her chair and kneeling beside Vince to examine Dek. "He sure hit the floor hard."

Vince stands up and returns to his cart. "He's awake but still paralyzed from the tranquilizer, so it shouldn't be a problem."

Stacy leans in close until she's a breath away from Dek's face. "I'm not sure you can hear me, but just so you know, it's nothing personal. I've been spying on this science research lab for a while, and your arrival offered me the chance to make some extra money. *Lots* of money!" she gloats with a shrill laugh.

Behind Stacy's leg Lauren opens her eyes to give Dek a quick wink before closing them again. He still can't move anything on his face and is glad she has regained some control of hers. The trank must be wearing off quicker for her.

Vince turns from his cart and returns to where Dek's lying, carrying a syringe, and flicking it with his finger. Dek guesses he's about to get another dose of whatever Stacy put in their drinks.

"Are you giving him another dose?" Stacy asks, moving back a little to give Vince better access to Dek while still allowing herself a view of the show.

Vince kneels next to Stacy over Dek who closes his eyes and prepares for the shot.

Suddenly, Stacy yells, "What the hell!"

Dek opens his eyes just as she slumps over him, partially covering his head. He can't see Vince, but he can hear him walking to some other part of the room. He must've drugged Stacy too. Then Dek notices Lauren has opened her eyes again. She mouths, *Concentrate.*

Dek gets it right away. Just like how they can heal or run faster or jump higher, maybe they can make their cells unblock their nerves and reverse the tranquilizer. That's what Lauren was doing earlier, and based on her mouth movement, it's working. So he closes his eyes and tries to concentrate. Though his head still hurts and is very foggy, he remembers what he learned in a yoga class he took with an old girlfriend years ago, breathing and focusing on communicating with his body.

Meanwhile, it sounds like Vince is going through Strong's office. He may be looking for the filter. "Finally! What a pain in the ass you've been," Dek hears him announce, assuming Vince has found it. He hears Vince come back to place it in a plastic bag on his cart before returning to Strong's office. Dek takes the opportunity to open his eyes and focus on trying to move his neck.

Lauren is now sitting up and seems to be back in good shape. She looks after Vince. "He's going around and picking things off different items in the rooms. Maybe he bugged this place too," she whispers. "Are you concentrating and trying to heal yourself?" She suddenly moves back into her old position as Vince comes back into the room.

"Just a little more cleanup, and I'll be out of your hair," Vince says jovially, setting something on his cart and walking back into the hallway.

Lauren pops up again and gives Dek an urgent look. "Are you getting better? I don't think we have much time left."

Dek is now able to free his head from under Stacy and push up on wobbly elbows, straining slightly under the extra weight. "I think I'm almost there. What's the plan?" he asks.

"We're the only two who can move right now. When I get an opening, I'll run for the door. He'll probably try to catch me, so you have to quickly come after us and knock him out of the way. Then we'll run for help."

"Okay, I think I can do that," Dek whispers, positioning himself back half under Stacy. With his hearing ramped up, he notices there's no heartbeat coming from Stacy. Could he be wrong, or is she dead? Furthermore, if Vince killed her even though she was working with him, what will do he with the rest of them?

Dek glances quickly at Lauren, trying to get her to notice Stacy's lack of a heartbeat, but she has her eyes closed again, pretending to be sedated. He hears Vince reenter the room and place some objects on his cart. He then walks back over to Dek, standing between Dek and Lauren. Dek stares up at Vince's malicious eyes but maintains the charade that he can't move.

"Mr. Thomas," Vince starts, gently pushing Stacy's limp body with his foot to have a better look at Dek's face. "You've been a greater challenge than I could have ever expected from your dossier. Intelligent but lazy and self-centered."

Dek can't tell if Vince is going to kill him or just smack-talk him.

"I'm not a science man, so I don't know what you've been experimenting on here with Dr. Strong or what has physically been going on with you, but I'm glad to be done with you," Vince says, pulling another syringe out of his pocket with a gloved hand.

Just then, the phone in Dr. Strong's office begins to ring. When Vince pauses and looks toward the office, Lauren uses the distraction to her advantage, jumping to her feet and shoving Vince over Stacy's corpse. He crashes to the ground with a grunt, and the syringe scatters across the floor. Lauren then tears for the door to the hallway, but Vince recovers quickly. Still on the ground, he begins to draw a gun from his janitor overalls, but Dek is up, kicking Vince across the face before he has a chance to do any damage.

Vince's head smacks against the ground, and the gun goes flying. "Fuck!"

Without looking back, Dek runs out the door and down the hallway after Lauren. They race down three flights of stairs, taking the steps two at a time. "Are you okay?" Dek asks as they reach the ground floor and explode into the lobby.

"Yeah," Lauren says, focusing on the front door. "Let's get out of here and call the cops."

They run to the front door and exit left, sprinting down the sidewalk toward the parking lot at the side of the building. Then Dek hears the soft spurt of a silenced gunshot and reflexively ducks as a bullet just misses his head and grazes Lauren's calf. She cries out in pain, falling on her side while clutching her bleeding leg. Dek grabs her and carries her the last forty feet to the corner leading to the parking lot, moving as fast as he can despite the drug still in his system. Three more shots are fired, but they miss.

"Hold on, Lauren!" Dek rasps as they round the corner, out of Vince's range, and run right into Richard who's getting out of his car and carrying a package. "Richard, thank God! Get back in the car and get us out of here!"

"Wait, why? What's going on?" Richard asks, trying to assess the scene. "Is Lauren hurt? What the hell, man?"

Dek grabs Richard's arm, turning him back to the car. "We were attacked at the lab. Everyone was knocked out, and that Vince guy from Madison was there. I think he may have killed Stacy. She was working with him. We barely escaped, and he shot Lauren in the leg." Dek talks a mile a minute as they quickly get in the car, Richard in the driver's seat and Dek in the back with Lauren to tend to her injured leg. "Richard, you have to get out of here *now*! We need to call the police. Give me your phone!" he yells. "We left the others up there so we could get help, but I don't think we have much time."

The tires squeal as Richard pulls out of the parking lot, turning left and away from the lab building. "Dek, are you sure you want to get the police involved?" he stammers, fishing for the phone in his coat pocket.

As he hands the phone back over his shoulder, an explosion shakes the car, and the phone falls to the floor. Dek and Lauren spin around to see the third floor of the building explode with a jet of fire lighting up the night sky. "No!" They cry, knowing their friends have most assuredly perished.

"Oh, shit, was that our lab?" Richard yells, looking back in the rearview mirror. "Dek, we need to talk about this before we go to the police. This is the second crazy lab accident you two have been involved in within the last two weeks."

Dek doesn't answer, just focuses on helping Lauren, stopping the bleeding by pressing a shirt he found in the backseat against the wound. Tears are streaming down Lauren's face, and Dek knows it has more to do with the loss of their friends than the injury to her leg.

"What are we going to do? Where are we going to go?" Lauren sobs.

Thinking for a moment, Dek finally tells Richard, "Head south toward Indy, Richard. I think I know of a place we can go where no one will know to look for us." Turning back to Lauren, he gently says, "Let's take a deep breath, regroup, and figure out our next step."

Lauren places her sweaty hand on his arm. "After what I just saw, I'm not sure the police could handle this. You don't need to keep pressure on my leg. I was able to stop the bleeding, and I can even somewhat keep the nerves from causing excessive pain if I concentrate. Hopefully, it's sunny tomorrow. Who knows, maybe I'll be good as new."

Dek removes his hand from her injury, giving her an exhausted half-smile. They both turn to the front of the car, staring out the window and trying to come to grips with what just happened.

CHAPTER 24

A darkly clothed Mr. Vincent exits the building out a side door as the blare of sirens echoes across the campus. He gets into a blue Chevy Suburban and casually tosses the plastic-wrapped filter into the passenger seat. He exits the parking lot, passing the oncoming emergency-response teams called in to manage the recent explosion. He disconnected then looped the university's security cameras the night before while placing the bugs in the lab, so they'll have a hard time deciding if this was anything other than an accident, especially with what little evidence he left at the scene.

Mr. Vincent plugs in his phone, and the dashboard display shows a map like a GPS map, but there are two cars showing up. One is miles from the other, traveling south toward Indianapolis. One is the car Mr. Vincent is driving.

He reaches up to rub his sore jaw. Mr. Thomas kicked him like a mule and almost knocked him unconscious. He may even have a concussion from his head hitting the floor. That can be the only reason he missed his shots from the window. Although, it looked like he got Miss Summers at least once in the leg. Maybe that will slow her down a bit. She moved like a cheetah back at the lab, and he wasn't ready for her to move at all, let alone like that. That stupid Stacy must not have drugged them good enough. The ones he gave her should've kept them all down for at least two hours.

What a mess! He was hoping to have this whole thing wrapped up with a nice little bow when he gave his next report to Helms. Now he'll have to tie up these loose ends before he can move on to his next assignment. He dials a number on his phone.

After about three rings, a voice comes through the car's speakers. "Do you have a favorable report?" Helms immediately asks.

"I have the filter, and Strong and his two lab assistants have been the victims of a terrible lab accident. I'm afraid they didn't survive."

"That's terrible," Helms replies dryly. "What about the other three?"

"The two primaries must not have gotten the full dose of the tranquilizer. They surprised me and got out before the explosion. Summers was injured. They met up with your son outside in the parking lot and fled the scene in his car. I have a tracker on that car and am following them south toward Indianapolis as we speak. I'll look for an opportune time to finish this."

"My *step*son," Helms says abruptly, correcting Mr. Vincent's error. "If the woman who bore him wasn't such a good person, I would've cut him free of our business long ago. Anyway, we're moving forward in South America. The mining teams are being deployed shortly. We need to have those loose ends tied up quickly and discreetly."

"I don't think Richard was fully aware of how serious this project is or the lengths we're willing to go to protect its integrity," Mr. Vincent adds. "If he's reluctant to continue on the path we've set forth, how should I proceed?"

"I should've known that idiot would never be able to handle such an important project. All I asked him to do was babysit Summers from afar, and he got himself all tangled up in our business," Helms growls. "If he isn't on board with how we've decided to proceed, we'll have no other choice. He'll need to be eliminated."

"I understand," Mr. Vincent replies apathetically. "I should be catching up with them shortly since they'll have to do something about Summers's injury. That will, no doubt, slow them down."

"We can't have them getting the police involved," Helms adds. "I'll send Richard a text, and we'll see if he's still in our corner."

"Yes, sir. Just let me know if something changes."

"I'm expecting this to be handled quickly, Mr. Vincent. I don't want any more excuses. Call me when everything's done," Helms says before disconnecting the call.

Mr. Vincent pulls into a McDonald's drive-through to grab dinner. When he has his burger and drink, he quickly parks to consult his digital map and plan out an intercept location. There's very little traffic at this time of night. If he can't catch up to them, he may have to get them in the morning. Taking a long sip of his drink, he exits the parking lot and heads south.

CHAPTER 25

"How's she doing?" Richard asks over his shoulder.

"She's resting," Dek replies, looking down at a sleeping Lauren, lying across the backseat with her legs elevated on his lap. "The bleeding's stopped, and I don't think the bone was fractured. We may need to make a pit stop at Walgreens to get some bandages and peroxide to clean and dress the area. If we can make it until morning, maybe the sun will help her heal. Let me know if you need to switch drivers. I don't think I can sleep after going through all that."

"I'm good for now. I'm pretty freaked out too. What happened back there?"

"I'm honestly not sure," Dek says, shaking his head and telling Richard everything he can remember.

"Did you say earlier that the janitor from Madison was there?" Richard asks.

"Yeah, isn't that insane? He must be some sort of tracker or hitman. He injected something into Stacy, and I think it killed her. I couldn't hear her heartbeat."

"What? He murdered her?" Richard exclaims, glancing back at Dek in the mirror.

"I'm pretty sure he killed Strong and Bobby too. We would've tried to get them out if we'd been back to one hundred percent.

We just weren't strong enough yet because of the trank," Dek says sadly. "I can't believe they're gone."

"It's not your fault, Dek," Richard says quietly. "Who could've guessed he would murder them?"

"After what happened to Stacy, I should've known!" Dek says angrily, causing Lauren to wake up.

She places a hand on his, pushing herself upright with a wince. "Where are we?" she asks, rubbing her eyes.

"Just north of Indianapolis," Richard says, "which is where we're going, right, Dek?"

"No, we still have a good ways to go. Down to Louisville and over to Lexington, then down to Knoxville and east toward Charlotte," Dek says.

"That'll take ten hours!"

"Yep, that's about right. I'm going to put as much distance between us and that killer as I can. I know a place we can stay just south of Charlotte that's off the map for most people. Now we need to look for a place to get some first-aid supplies to get that leg cleaned up." He gives Lauren's hand a gentle squeeze.

"Once we get to this secret location, are we calling the cops? What's the plan going forward?" Richard asks.

"We have to find a way to get help," Dek says. "Having just been a part of our second major lab accident in three weeks, I think we could easily be considered suspects rather than victims."

Lauren checks something on her phone. "The news is saying there was a fatal accident at a lab facility on the Northwestern campus. There may have been shots fired, but there are conflicting witness accounts. The police are searching for other suspects who may have fled the scene."

"'Fatal accident,'" Dek repeats. "There's probably little chance that Vince was one of the fatalities. He must've had something on his janitor's cart to cause the explosion. We pushed right by it. We could have stopped all this."

"Or we could be dead too," Lauren adds.

"There!" Richard says pointing to a Walgreens just up ahead.

"Great, I'll go in and get the supplies and some food for the drive. Just hang tight; I'll be right back," Dek tells Lauren, easing out from under her legs and running inside the store.

**

As soon as Dek's in the door, Richard turns to Lauren. "If you're okay, I'm going to touch base with my parents. They may be worried after the accident." He leaves the car running and walks over next to the side of the building to make his call.

The phone only rings once before Helms picks up on the other end. "Hey, what happened? Are you still with the other two scientists?" he asks quickly.

"Don't you mean, 'Are you okay?'" Richard asks. "What the hell, Helms? That maniac you had following us just killed *three* people and blew up the lab!"

"Are you out in a public place? Keep your voice down!" Helms hisses. "I told you if we didn't get that filter quickly, I would have to take things in a different direction."

"What if I was there? I could have been injured," Richard whines.

"That's why I sent you on your little journey to pick up the container," Helms replies sternly. "Now quit whining! Are you still with Summers and Thomas?"

"Yes, Lauren's been shot! We're getting some supplies right now. This is getting way out of hand!" Richard says, starting to panic.

"Calm down; we don't have much time. Try to keep them from going to the police. Where are you going?" Helms says, quickly trying to take advantage of the little time they have.

"Don't even think of sending that guy after us!"

"No, no," Helms says reassuringly. "I'm making up a proposal for the two of them. I'll give them money and a way out of this in exchange for them keeping quiet about what little they know of our activities."

"I don't think they'll go for that," Richard says. "But I guess it's worth a try. I think we're going someplace south of Charlotte, but I'm not sure where."

"Hey man, let's get going!" Dek yells as he emerges from the store.

"Oh yeah, I'm just touching base with my family," Richard says, putting his hand over the phone. "I've got to go. Talk to you later. Love you too." He quickly ends the call and jogs back to the car.

Dek's cleaning Lauren's leg and putting on a bandage. They exchange a private look of concern over Richard's phone call. "It still looks bad," Dek says, wrapping a bandage around Lauren's calf. "Lots of inflammation, but I still think it was a clean wound. I don't think he got the bone."

Richard slides back behind the wheel, and Dek climbs into the passenger seat, leaving the entire back for Lauren to rest. "Let's make some time and put some distance between us and that lunatic back in Chicago," Dek says, patting his hand on the dash. He gives Richard a strained smile, handing him a granola bar he bought in the store, and they pull out to continue their route south.

CHAPTER 26

The guys decide to change drivers when they stop for gas near Louisville. Dek takes over, and Richard, who says he isn't feeling well, rests his eyes in the passenger seat. After about two more hours, they find a small motel off the highway about thirty minutes north of the Tennessee border called the Overlook Inn. It's a small, ten-unit motel positioned right next to a vast scenic overlook across the street from a sheer drop-off of over one hundred feet. They check into two separate rooms, one for Richard and one for Lauren and Dek. The rooms are small with two queen beds and a bathroom. There's a small table and one chair located in front of the only window next to the door. From the window, they can look out over a beautiful valley with a rolling mountain backdrop. Richard's room is two doors down on the right.

"This has been one of the craziest days of my life," Richard says after helping Dek get Lauren inside and situated on the bed. "I can sure use a little sleep."

"Hey, Richard," Dek says. "Thank you for everything. I don't know what we would've done without your help tonight."

Richard gives them a half-smile. "No problem," he says, offering a small wave and closing the door as he leaves.

Dek lies next to Lauren on the bed they decide to share. They look at each other, silently listening to Richard unlock the door to his room and go inside.

"Any chance this room is bugged?" Lauren asks, trying to make a bad joke.

"Looking at the condition of our room and the *interesting* smell of the place, I'd say there's a good chance that this bed may be *bugged*," Dek replies with a bad joke of his own. "I don't think anyone could possibly know we'd be stopping here. It's completely random. I've never stopped here before, and we paid with cash. By the way, what was Richard doing back at the pharmacy while I was getting supplies?" he asks quietly, still feeling like someone's constantly listening in on them.

"He said he was calling his family to let them know he was okay. Did you hear any of the conversation when you came out of the store?"

"A little. I think he was saying where we're going, but I guess that's expected if your family's worried."

"I'm getting a bad feeling about this," Lauren says. "Richard isn't lying to us, but I get the vibe that he's hiding something. He went with Stacy to get the food but somehow got sidetracked and didn't get back for two hours. I know I've asked you this before, but really, how well do you know him?"

"Not that well actually," Dek replies, thinking back. "We've only been sharing the same lab for the last four months. To be honest, we don't really have a lot in common other than science. He doesn't go out, doesn't like sports ... I don't know what he does in his spare time. He always seemed to have a big hang-up with his stepfather though. On the one hand, he'd brag about how much money they had and the fact that his stepfather runs a big company. On the other, he was always complaining about the control his stepfather has over his life and career decisions."

"So, you guys basically just shared lab space until he somehow decided to help you out with this trip across America as you run from the law? I'm feeling less and less convinced that he has good intentions."

"That's true ... and in Chicago, he was asking about having us infect him with the virus. Maybe he's been tagging along this whole time because he thinks we're on to some big money-making discovery. Once he found out about the virus, he's been looking for a piece of the action."

"Infect him with the virus? Is he crazy? You saw what happened to his sample. There's a high chance that it could kill him!"

"Richard said his stepfather sent him to pick up a package. He was carrying something when we ran into him. Maybe it's for his business or something," Dek says, starting to relax and feeling very tired.

"What kind of business does his stepdad do?" Lauren asks, more awake after having slept for most of the car ride.

Yawning, Dek says, "He owns a big chemical company or something like that. My friend James did an internship for them last year but didn't like the direction the company was going, so he didn't apply for a job."

"James? Is that the big guy who popped in on us at your house the other day?"

"Yep, he's pretty much my best friend," Dek says as his eyes start closing.

"Can you call him? Right now? I want to know what company Richard's stepfather owns. What if Richard's somehow tied to all of this?"

"Now? It's nighttime, so he's probably sleeping," Dek deflects, not interested in making any late-night or early-morning calls.

"Come on, what if I'm on to something?" Lauren urges, pushing his arm.

"Okay, okay, I'll try him," Dek moans, grabbing his phone. "He's probably going to be pissed at me for not calling earlier."

After a few rings, a sleepy-sounding James picks up the phone. "Dek, is that you, man? What's up? You all right?"

"Hey, bud. Sorry for hitting you up in the middle of night. We're fine, but I've been put through the wringer this week. I have a quick question for you."

"Wait a minute, am I still asleep or did you just say, 'we're fine'? Is that girl still with you?"

Dek laughs and rolls his eyes. "Yeah, her name's Lauren, and believe it or not, she's still here. What was the name of the company that you interned for last year? The one Richard's stepdad was with."

"Oh, that was Helms Chemical Development, but they were changing all their focus. It was all very hush-hush, but I talked to a guy involved in purchasing who gave me the scoop. I think they were trying to get government weapon contracts, using radiation signatures and chemical components to make smart bombs. I wasn't interested in any of that. Did they offer you or Lauren an internship?"

"Helms Chemical Development, huh?" Dek repeats so Lauren can hear the name. "No, I just couldn't remember the name, and it came up in conversation."

"At this hour, I would hope you two were having a different kind of conversation, if you know what I mean."

"Very funny, and thanks, man. How are things going back home?"

"We're all good, but have you heard there was a fire at the lab where you were injured? How's your hand by the way?"

"I did hear about the fire. Crazy that it happened right after our accident," Dek says, glancing at Lauren who's typing away on her phone. "You won't believe how great my hand is healing up. I need to show you some of the gains I've been making at the gym. I may finally be able to keep up with you."

"Sounds good. When are you guys coming home?" James asks.

"We're still trying to sort out a few things, so it may be a while," Dek says, trying not to be overly committal. The last thing he wants is to get James involved.

"Well be safe, my friend. I got to get back to sleep. Got an early day tomorrow. I'll see you soon."

"Thanks. Say hi to Pam for me. We'll talk again soon," Dek promises before disconnecting the call. He looks over at Lauren and can tell right away from her determined expression he's not getting any sleep soon. "What did you find out about the company?"

"I'm not sure, but I think the samples I was working on were for a chemical company because of the way they were packaged when they arrived. It wasn't the standard mineral sample packaging. Something about it just looked more like the packaging that the chemical I used to clean the samples came in. I don't know … what would a chemical company need with a radioactive metal?"

"James just told me that Helms Chemical was trying to branch out in a new direction—military weapons development."

"That's got to be it!" Lauren exclaims, slapping her phone down on the bed. "I had a distinct feeling about those samples. A radioactive signal that specific would definitely have a military application."

"So, what does this mean about Richard?" Dek asks cautiously, taking them back to their original concern.

"I think it means he was telling Vince where we are and what we were doing, allowing him to spy on us to get that filter back and maybe even kill us," Lauren says.

Dek pauses for a second. "Judging by his response, I don't think Richard knew about the drugging at the lab or that Vince was going to kill anyone. But I do think he may be feeding information about us to his stepfather and Vince."

"That has to be why he insisted on helping us that night at the lab in Madison. To keep tabs on us."

"If he's passing information to Vince, then they know where we are and are heading this way now," Dek says, hopping up from the bed and getting their things together, suddenly wide awake.

"Let's go have a talk with our 'friend' down the hall," Lauren says, carefully lowering her injured leg to stand up.

After they gather all their things together, they make their way to Richard's room. Dek knocks firmly on the door. "Richard, you have to get up. We need to get out of here."

Richard opens the door. "What's going on? I thought we were going to try and sleep. I'm still not feeling too good," he says, yawning.

Dek pushes past him into the room with his free hand, holding Lauren against him with his arm. He eases her down on the bed, then turns back to Richard. "What does your stepfather's company do?" he asks, getting straight to the point.

Richard is instantly awake, and Dek can see the wheels turning as Richard looks between him and Lauren. He's trying to figure out what they may know and is preparing a lie.

"It's Helms Chemical Development. They make cleaners and other commercial products. What're you getting at?" Richard asks defensively.

Lauren leans forward. "Any weapons development? I think it was your stepdad's company that commissioned me to test the samples that caused the accident, and I think this crazy murderer who's following us works for them too."

Again, Richard looks between the two of them, feigning shock. "I don't know what you're talking about," he says, backing up and shaking his head. He's clearly flustered and truly does not look well—pale skin, dark sunken eyes.

"Richard, we know you're lying," Dek says, crossing his arms.

Richard turns toward the door and hits his head against it three times. "Okay, look, this has all gone way too far." After a short pause, he continues. "I was just supposed to watch Lauren and make sure everything was done properly and without any commotion." He keeps his head against the door with his back to them. "I sent Dek up to the lab the day of the accident because he was being a douche, and I knew the samples had been sent off. I just thought you would yell at him and maybe get him into trouble. But, of course, you two have an accident and draw all kinds of attention to the area. The company sent Vince in to clean up the mess and keep things quiet. I had no idea what that meant or to what extent he would take it. When I happened to see you two together at the apartment, I got worried that Lauren would tell some of our secrets to explain the accident. So, I followed you to the lab and tried to tag along after we escaped the storage room."

"You knew the janitor was working for your stepfather's company when he locked us in that storage closet?" Dek yells.

Richard slowly turns to face them, tears forming in his bloodshot eyes. "At the time, I didn't know who he was, and I never believed we were in any danger."

Lauren's stunned to actually hear the truth come out of Richard's mouth but also feels a little vindicated that what she'd believed was true.

"Richard, I can't believe you actually had a hand in all of this," Dek says, shaking his head. "Did you know when you left Strong's office to get food that Vince was going to kill us?"

"What? No! Dek, I swear. I didn't even know that Stacy was working with Vince." Richard pauses to get out a coughing spell. "I got a call from my stepdad as we were leaving the lab, asking me to run an errand for him. When I got back, I ran into you two outside. I had *no idea* that Vince was going to hurt anyone." Tears are now freely running down Richard's face, his voice strained. "You've got to believe me, Dek. I thought he just wanted that stupid filter!"

Lauren's sitting with her head in her hands, and Dek slumps down next to her, resting his arm across her back. "They died because we came to them for help," Lauren says quietly. She then suddenly stiffens, lifting her head. "Did you hear that?"

Dek nods.

A car door just quietly closed in the parking lot outside.

"What is it?" Richard asks, panic rising in his voice. He slides the curtain corner back and peeks out.

"No!" Lauren and Dek yell as Dek reaches for Richard.

The window cracks and the back of Richard's head explodes, spraying blood and bone matter across the end of the bed.

Dek jumps back, pushes Lauren off the other side of the bed, and dives to the ground as many more bullets pierce the broken window and the door.

Richard's body has slumped to the ground, partially blocking the door.

After a few seconds, the shooting stops, and Dek can hear the click of the empty cartridge being ejected from a gun on the other side of the door. *It's now or never*, he thinks, preparing for a fight. But the welcome sound of a distant siren echoes through the mountain pass.

"Goddamn it!" He hears someone yell as the sirens get closer. A new clip is in place, so the assailant tries the door. However, it only opens an inch since Richard's body is blocking it. Dek spins around and kicks it shut, then rolls toward the side wall. A spray of silenced bullets tears though the door again, over half of the bullets slicing Richard's corpse.

Dek hears the sirens enter the motel parking lot. A car door opens, and someone shouts, "Drop the gun!"

Some silenced shots and two return shots go off. Someone groans and calls on the radio for backup. Then a car door slams and tires squeal as it peels away.

Dek chances a glance out the window and sees a black sedan speed out of the parking lot, heading north. He jumps across the bed, looking for Lauren. "Are you okay?"

"Yeah, I think so," she replies, pulling herself up off the floor and grabbing Richard's keys from the stand next to the bed. "We have to get out of here."

Dek wraps his arm around Lauren, and they push Richard's body out of the way before peering out over the parking lot. A police car is sitting about thirty yards away with the lights flashing and the driver's door open. A man's body is lying on the ground behind the door, which has been riddled with bullets. Dek takes Lauren to Richard's car and eases her into the passenger seat. "I'm going to check on the officer before we go," he says, shutting her door before she can argue.

The officer is conscious and bleeding from his left shoulder.

"Are you okay?" Dek asks, leaning over him, using part of his shirt to conceal his face.

"Yeah, I'm good. Got more friendlies on the way," the officer says, his hand clutching his injured shoulder.

"Thanks," Dek says, patting the cop's good shoulder. "You saved us. I'll get more help." He uses this as a good excuse to leave, running back to Richard's car and heading south. In the rearview mirror, he can see the officer standing next to his car now, watching them leave. "That was miracle timing," he says, trying to catch his breath. "If that cop hadn't pulled up at that exact time, I don't know if I would've been able to overpower our assailant. That had to be Vince again. I'm pretty sure I recognized his voice."

Lauren's sitting stunned in the passenger seat. "Richard's dead," she whispers. "All these deaths because I took a contract I knew wasn't from a legitimate source. I brought all this on us ... for *money*."

Dek reaches over and takes her hand. "We all do everything we can to get ahead in life. You had an opportunity and took it," he says, trying to comfort her. "I think the important thing now is to survive and then do whatever we can to set things right."

"Yeah, I guess ..." she replies, still slightly shaken.

"Why don't you try to rest? I'm not feeling at all tired after the last two hours. I'll be fine to drive. Once we get to Knoxville, we can leave this car in a lot and rent something for the rest of the trip. As soon as we can get to a safe place, we'll decide how we want to go to the police."

Lauren pushes her seat back and turns toward the window. Dek can tell she won't be able to sleep either, but at least she can get some rest before sunrise.

CHAPTER 27

It's a truly welcome sight to see the sun as it rises over the Smoky Mountains. For a moment, Dek and Lauren forget everything they're running from and just enjoy the view. In Knoxville, they get some food and leave Richard's car in a strip mall parking area. They're able to rent a Toyota Camry and get right back on the road. After a few fairly silent hours of driving, they enter North Carolina and start a very scenic part of their trip.

Lauren's the first to break the silence. "In the past twenty-four hours, we've lost four of our friends," she says solemnly, staring out the front windshield, almost talking to herself as much as to Dek. "I feel so sad but also so relieved to be alive. That you're still alive and here with me."

Dek glances over at her as he drives.

"I know Stacy and Richard had other motivations that didn't align with ours, or with our safety for that matter, but we knew them and had experiences with them, and now they're dead. Not to mention Dr. Strong and sweet Bobby; they in no way deserved to die. I just don't know how to process the losses mentally. I don't know how I should be feeling. Should I be crying over the deaths or rejoicing the fact that we made it out?" she asks, still staring straight ahead.

"Any life lost is a tragedy," Dek says quietly. "Losing friends or even acquaintances is always going to be hard to process. We can't change what's happened. We can honor those lives by continuing and finding out where this path leads. We can bring to light what happened to them and, hopefully, find justice for the man who killed them. We have to stay strong. We have each other and need to cherish every moment this life gives us," he finishes, reaching over to take her hand.

They drive for a few minutes, weaving their way through the mountains and trying to get a glimpse of the fabulous views as they fly by. "Hey, Dek, pull over at the next rest stop that has a scenic overlook," Lauren says, pointing to a blue rest stop sign.

They pull in and get out to stretch. The stop is just a small parking area with spots to accommodate about six cars and a picnic bench perfect for a family snack. Dek puts his arm around Lauren to help her get out of the car. "How's the leg?" he asks, hoping she's not in too much pain.

"I've been using my time in the car to focus on healing," Lauren says before pointing to another blue sign next to a narrow, heavily wooded path. "Let's go up that path and have a look."

They limp up the path, and after about fifty feet, the path opens into a small clearing the size of a standard living room. There's a large, flat rock surface, and on the far side of the clearing is a drop-off overlooking an expansive valley. As far as they can see, the view is trees and mountainsides—no houses, buildings, or roads. It makes Dek think this must've been the same view enjoyed by early explorers before the industrial revolution. The bright sun coats them in warmth as he helps Lauren sit down on the rock. He plops down next to her, gazing out over the valley. The more he focuses, the more his eyes can see everything so clearly. He points out an owl's nest on a far tree. Glancing back at Lauren, he sees she's lying back on the rock with her shirt pulled up, exposing her perfect, pale stomach.

He guesses he may have paused too long to admire her because she turns to him with a sly smile and says, "The view is the other way. I can feel the sun's effect so strongly up here. I was hoping the elevation would help my healing."

"Is it?" he asks, checking her bandage. "Should we take a look at how it's healing?"

"Sure, why not? Maybe direct sunlight on the wound will help it heal faster, stimulate the cells," Lauren says, propping up on her elbow to get a better look.

Dek carefully removes the bandage and gauze. There's only a small remnant of dried blood on the gauze. "I guess we don't need this anymore," he says, holding up the used pad. There's a mark on the skin, but the wound has completely closed, and new skin is forming on the surface. "Wow!" he says gently touching her leg. "It's already almost completely healed."

"Internally, I still have some healing to do. That bullet tore through my calf muscle, and it may take more of this amazing sunlight to be able to run like I did a few days ago," Lauren says.

Dek lies back on the rock next to Lauren, resting on his left side and watching her stare up at the wispy cloud formations drifting above them. She peeks over at him. "Again, I believe the scenic view is that way," she says with a slight nod toward the valley.

"Speak for yourself. This is the view I'm most interested in," he says, leaning toward her. He reaches over, placing his hand gently in her hair at the base of her neck. After a beat, he kisses her softly at first, then a little more passionately. He hears her sigh a little and thinks they've both been anticipating their first kiss for some time. It feels incredibly right. He doesn't know if it's the sun, the scene, or just the girl, but it's the best kiss he's ever experienced. Needing to breathe, he pulls back slightly and sees a warm smile stretch across Lauren's face.

"You can kiss me like that again whenever you like," she purrs, reaching around his neck to pull him in.

They kiss for several minutes before they hear other hikers coming up the path. Dek gently pulls back, sitting up. "I think we've run out of privacy," he says with a smile. He sneaks in one more quick kiss before helping Lauren up, and they walk hand-in-hand back down the path to the car.

"What's the plan?" she asks, still smiling at him from the passenger's seat.

Dek pulls out of the rest area and continues east toward Charlotte. "Once we get to Charlotte, we'll return this rental car and get a ride to our next location. It's about forty minutes south of Charlotte. I don't want to leave a clear path as to where our final destination is in case anyone's tracking us."

"And where is our final destination?" Lauren asks, leaning over to give him a kiss on the cheek.

"For now, I'll keep it a surprise," he says with a wink. "We need to have a minute to rest, heal, and organize our next steps. I'm hoping I have just the place."

CHAPTER 28

When they get to Charlotte and turn in the rental car, they order an Uber to take them to a restaurant called the Wagon Wheel south of Charlotte in South Carolina. It has an actual wagon wheel on the sign out front. After an amazing lunch of real Southern chicken and dumplings with a side of fried squash, they order a Lift to their final destination only about five minutes down the road. Dek hopes if they use multiple rideshares and don't end at their exact destination, maybe they can cover their tracks.

They turn down a small road directly off the highway. There are lots of small doublewide houses and trailers lining the route. The road takes a hard right, and a lake comes into view. Fishing Creek Reservoir is a small lake on the Catawba River. It's about five miles long and barely a mile wide at its widest point. It's sparsely populated, located between Lake Wylie and Lake Wateree, two much larger lakes. They travel about one hundred feet before Dek indicates for the driver to let them out.

"I didn't even know this was down here," the driver says as they get out before turning around and heading back.

"Is this it?" Lauren asks Dek, staring through the tall trees toward the lake.

"Almost," he replies. "Just up the hill on the lakeside. I didn't want the driver to drop us at the actual location, just to be careful."

He helps Lauren up a small hill to a little one-story gray house with a large porch on the side, overlooking the lake. There's a green Camry parked out front and a No Trespassing sign in the window.

"Do you know the people who live here?" Lauren asks, eyeing the car.

"No one lives here," he replies, heading up the front walk toward the porch. "This is my dad's lake house. That car used to be mine, but he just stores it here so the house appears lived in. He loves the lake and keeps it as a second house. It looks like he hasn't been down here for a couple of weeks. The grass is looking pretty long."

Dek picks up a fake rock near the steps to the porch and grabs the extra key hiding under it. He holds the screen door open with a large rock and unlocks the door. Lauren limps past him to a deck that extends back from the porch toward the lake. He goes inside and turns on the window air conditioners. He opens the front windows to let in some fresh air as the ACs hum to life.

Lauren's standing at the top of the deck and realizes the best views of the lake are up there. From that position, the deck leads down along the back of the house to a massive lower deck with sun chairs and a couch, a perfect area for entertaining guests. The lower deck is surrounded by a cascade of steps leading to the lake. The house sits on about an acre of land with one hundred feet of shoreline and is elevated on a hill about thirty feet from the shore, allowing for a beautiful view of the lake. There is a large, rectangular, floating dock with a jet ski attached to the side of the lower deck.

"What do you think?" Dek asks, walking up behind Lauren. He puts his hands on the railing on either side of hers and nestles his head on her shoulder.

"It's really beautiful, Dek," she says, putting a hand on his. "Do you really think we'll be safe?"

"I don't know," he admits. "That Vince guy is after us. We have to decide in the next few days what we're going to do."

Lauren turns around in his arms and wraps her arms around his neck, giving him another amazing kiss. "Is there a shower?" she asks, ducking under his arms and walking back to the doorway. "Nice rock!" she says with a laugh, looking down at the makeshift door stop.

"It adds to the rustic feel of the house," he says, laughing and following her inside.

Lauren enters the house into the main living area with two couches positioned around an old TV. The kitchen is attached to the living room, separated by a four-foot peninsula countertop. The kitchen is spacious with a fridge, sink, and stove. There are two bedrooms and a full bathroom at the back of the house. At the front of the house is a wall of windows overlooking the lake with two sitting areas separated by a dining table. Clearly the best part of the house.

Lauren's enjoying the front views of the lake while Dek checks out the fridge. "Jackpot!" he says, emerging with two beers. "My dad, being from Wisconsin originally, would never forget to stock a fridge with beer."

They crack open their beers and sit down in the front room to enjoy the view of the lake for a while.

After finishing her beer, Lauren sets it down on the side table, then reaches down and takes off her bandage. The bullet wound, less than twenty-four hours old, is almost entirely healed. She moans as she attempts to stretch the calf out. "It's still very stiff and swollen," she says, massaging the area, "but a lot better than yesterday."

"The skin around the wound looks just like my hand did when it was first healing," Dek says, looking at his replaced digits. Even today, the skin still looks newer and feels smooth like a baby's bottom.

"Is that an island out there?" Lauren asks, pointing to a large, forested piece of land about one hundred yards out on the lake.

"Yep, we called it Snake Island when I was a kid. Not that we ever saw any snakes on it. I think we just thought it sounded ominous. There's a rusted truck and some old appliances out there. I guess, at one time, someone bought the land to build a house on it but found out that you can't build on an island in a public waterway. So, they just left some of their things there rather than taking the effort to bring it back to shore. I'm not sure if any of that's true, but the stuff's still out there," he explains.

"It looks very thick," Lauren says, still gazing out across the water.

"You'd be surprised," he says. "The bank of the island slopes up about three or four feet, then levels out. That's just the bank rising up that you see from here, and the flat part is very open with these gigantic trees forming a canopy over some lower ground cover. It's actually really cool when you're up on top, but there are lots of insects and probably snakes."

"We should take a trip over there," Lauren says. "It sounds fun, and you said there are some kayaks and paddleboards under the house. We can try it out when my leg's fully healed."

"Speaking of that, let's put some beers in a cooler and go chill out on the dock in the sun to ramp up that healing process," Dek suggests, getting up and heading to the kitchen to set up a cooler. "I think there are some swimsuits in the back rooms if you need one ...." He trails off, looking up and seeing Lauren has already stripped down to her bra and panties and is out the door. "Or you could go just like that," he says, a large grin stretching across his face.

It's been about eight years since Dek has spent any significant time at the lake, and he forgot how wonderful it can be. He has such fond memories of fishing with his dad and little brother, kayaking and jet skiing until nightfall. His father used to pull him and his brother on a tube behind their jet ski and whip the two of them off only to have them both pop out of the water, screaming for another ride. He has never brought a girl here before, and watching Lauren sunbathing on the dock, he thinks this may be the perfect first girl to share the experience with. He gets some towels and chairs and joins Lauren on the dock. The sun feels amazing as they relax and talk and enjoy the rest of the afternoon.

Around 6 p.m., the sun starts to fall behind the house, so they clean up the dock and head back to the house to get dressed and eat some dinner. When their cells work overtime, they become famished. Dek throws a frozen pizza in the oven and sets up a fire pit on the lower patio. It doesn't take long before the pizza's ready, and they eat their dinner and enjoy the fire while sitting out on the couch positioned on the lower deck, looking out over the lake.

"This is really amazing, Decklan," Lauren whispers, easing closer to him and resting her head on his shoulder.

Dek puts his arm around her and kisses the top of her head. "You're amazing. This has been the craziest time of my life, and I'm scared as hell that this won't end well, but it's all worth it having found you."

He then sets up a small speaker and plays some Dave Matthews music. They enjoy the rest of the night by the fire, making love for the first time and watching a full moon rise over the lake. With their senses stronger than ever, they can fully experience every second of their time together. Once they finish, Dek rolls over and drifts off to sleep, feeling as if his whole body is smiling.

CHAPTER 29

Mr. Vincent's gathering his clothes together and packing up his small suitcase. This simple job has turned into a giant headache. He takes time to check his firearm, freshly cleaned and ready to go. He failed to kill Thomas and Summers at the hotel. How that cop was able to appear out of nowhere, he'll never know. Better to not take the risk of getting caught. He'll have a second chance to get all these loose ends tied up soon enough.

He checked the local news in Lexington and saw there was only mention of a drug deal gone wrong and one casualty at the motel. That means the kids got away before the police could question them. But oddly, there was no mention of the officer who was shot at the scene. At least there's less publicity. Keep it quiet and get the job done quickly and cleanly. That's what he was taught. Unfortunately, this job has been nothing of the sort. Somehow, two complete amateurs have managed to mess up his plans at every turn. If he can't get the situation under control quickly, he'll lose all the credibility he's worked so hard to build.

Suddenly, his phone vibrates in his pocket. He knows who's on the other end of the line and isn't sure what kind of reaction Richard's killing will invoke from his stepfather. "Sir," Mr. Vincent answers, always a professional.

"I hope all the crap that I'm going through over the death of my stepson means the situation's been fully rectified," Helms growls into the phone. "The Kentucky police told us he was the only one checked into his room and that he died alone. They suspect the killer took his car, which they later discovered near Knoxville. I heard no mention of the deaths of his two companions. Am I to assume you took care of them some other way the police have yet to discover?"

Mr. Vincent allows Helms to get it all out before replying. "The other two got away when a police officer arrived and called in backup as I was making my move. I thought it was more important to leave the scene rather than be caught or get into a large shootout with the police. Did the police who contacted you mention that an officer was hurt at the scene?"

"No, nothing like that, just that Richard was found dead in his room, and some baggies of meth were found in the parking lot outside his room. They believe it was a drug deal, and that Richard stiffed the other guy and then ran into his room to hide. He was killed through the window near the door." Helms pauses allowing for a response. "Was that not close to how it went down?"

"Close enough," Mr. Vincent replies.

"The odd part is that the coroner's report said Richard had stage-four lung cancer. We had no idea of his condition, but it works for us. That makes it look even more likely that he was seeking drugs to deal with the cancer pain."

"I also wasn't aware of Richard having cancer. Lucky coincidence."

"This doesn't sound like all of the loose ends have been tied up," Helms says with more than a hint of anger in his voice.

"No, sir, I'm still pursuing the other two. Our previous intel had them somewhere south of Charlotte, North Carolina. I arrived in Charlotte this morning and have set up a hotel on the south side of town. I believe I'm within an hour's drive of their location and am prepared to move once I've located them."

"Richard did say something about Charlotte in our last conversation," Helms replies. "If you fail to take care of this situation again, I'll have to call in someone else, Mr. Vincent. This won't look good in regards to you and your future working for this company, or possibly any company. I'm on a strict timetable. Feldman has already been dispatched to Ecuador to oversee the mining project, so we cannot afford any more failures."

"Yes sir, I understand," Mr. Vincent says dryly. "I'll speed up my plans."

"See that you do. You've had a very successful run with this company over the last couple of years. You wouldn't want to become one of the loose ends we so often need tied up," Helms adds menacingly before disconnecting the call.

Mr. Vincent calmly hangs up the phone and uses his laptop to search for any information he can find on the incident in Kentucky. It's just as Helms described. A University of Wisconsin researcher was found dead in a hotel room in Kentucky, an apparent drug deal gone bad. No mention of an officer being hurt at the scene or details about the confrontation. This almost looks like someone's doing the sort of work Mr. Vincent does—cleaning up the evidence. Could Helms already have another team on the case? Mr. Vincent has to keep the possibility in mind as he proceeds with his plans. If the other team finds the targets before him, he'll be out a big payday. He must find Thomas and Summers quickly.

Mr. Vincent next types in a search for Badger Rental. After a short phone call, he sits back in his chair, monitoring his computer for any hits on Thomas's or Summers's phone.

***

A convoy of heavily laden supply trucks plunges through the Ecuadorian jungle. The road has been well traveled over the past few weeks and worn smooth by the large tires of the Helms Chemical mining crew and all the necessary equipment for the setup of a mining basecamp.

The camp is about a half-square-mile long in the shape of a rectangle and located to the east of the Andes Mountains along the Napo River just north of Yasuní National Park. They're set up only fifty miles from the Colombian border, the exact location where the earlier mining discovery team only found tainted samples of metal.

The convoy emerges from the forest as the road continues down the center of the camp. At first, the road is lined on either side by giant earth movers. There are four parked on each side of the road, facing the center, a very intimidating entrance. Next, there's a line of barracks, five on each side of the road. They're shiny metal tubes looking to be half-submerged in the earth. Each barrack is fifty feet long and has double wooden doors on either end, which are currently open to allow maximum airflow, with mosquito netting offering some protection from the bugs.

At the end of the road is a large basecamp headquarters building. It looks like a camping lodge with wooden walls and a flight of stairs leading up to two large double doors. The road splits at the headquarters building and diverges into two parking areas on either side.

The convoy enters the parking area to the right and lines up to have their cargo dispatched to the camp. A group of men follow the convoy in and begin to unload the supplies. The passenger door of the lead truck swings open, and Feldman's tall, lanky frame makes an awkward descent to the newly cleared jungle floor. After a few failed attempts to shoo away the clouds of bugs and dust, he hurries for the protection of the headquarters office space.

"I'll put your things in barrack one," the driver yells after him, nudging one of the other men as they laugh at Feldman's ridiculous retreat from nature.

Once inside, Feldman wastes little time getting his computer and work area set up.

"Captain Santiago, I need a status update. How are we progressing? When can we begin to mine the metal?"

"Sir, we've run into a few snags," Captain Santiago says, nervously crimping his hat in his hands.

"What sort of snags?" Feldman asks, not bothering to look up from his computer. "Dammit!" he shouts before Santiago can answer, unplugging and replugging his satellite connection. "Sorry. What snags?" he repeats, finally looking up.

"Well, there are some superstitions that many of the local workers fear when it comes to mining in this area. They don't want to dig here," he says with a deep Ecuadorian accent.

"What a bunch of shit!" Feldman replies, blowing off the validity of the statement and resuming his computer setup.

"The men said there was a small group of twenty miners who were looking for gold in the caves just north of the river. More than half of the group died within a week of starting their dig. The men say the land is poisoned and must not be disturbed."

"They probably ran into some toxic fumes. I'm sure they didn't have proper ventilation or the appropriate protective gear. We'll be supplying both. There should be nothing to fear," Feldman says. "Ah-ha! At last, a connection. Gather the men outside in an hour, and I'll address their concerns. Time is money, and we need to get this operation up and running."

After an intense discussion with the crew, Feldman manages to bring most of the men to his side before returning to his office for a final planning session with Santiago. "There was one older man named Lupé who seemed to be a major player in this poisoned land nonsense," Feldman says. "Constantly raving about how a group of three miners and a researcher got sick while digging for metallurgic materials some fourteen years ago. Only one of them survived the sickness, and he seems to think our mining project could have similar results. He'll need to be moved to a different detail where he can have a less direct impact on the feelings of the group. Put him on the transport team and keep him near the airport. Most of the younger men seem to be okay, especially after I mentioned a bonus for being ahead of schedule."

"Yes sir, I would agree most are very motivated by money," Santiago replies, taking notes on a small pad.

"If some start to die, we'll have to order higher-quality protective gear. We need to keep the project moving." Feldman walks to the back door of the office, looking through the mosquito netting out into the jungle. "Poisoned or not, the show *will* go on."

CHAPTER 30

Dek wakes up with a start. He was having a dream about that night in the motel, the night of Richard's death. This time, the cops didn't come, and Vince was aiming his gun at Lauren. It was the feeling of losing Lauren that woke him with such intensity. He immediately looks for her on the other side of the bed, but she's gone.

"Good morning, sleepy head," Lauren says from the door. She's wearing one of the shirts Dek's dad left for guests and sipping on a cup of coffee. "Did you have a bad dream?" she asks, coming in and sitting next to him on the edge of the bed.

"I don't know if I'm ever not going to have bad dreams after all this," he says grimly as he falls back onto his pillow and wraps his arms around Lauren's waist, hugging her midsection. "I know this sounds crazy, but I now feel like I have something to lose, and that's a scary concept for me."

"I take it *I'm* that something," she says, looking down at him with a smile. She sets her coffee cup on the side table and slides into bed. "I kind of feel the same way," she says, kissing him lovingly.

He slides her shirt off, tossing it onto the floor, and they make love again, trying to forget all the trouble and chaos and pain of the last two weeks by enjoying a few more hours of ecstasy.

Afterward, they lie in bed, their legs still intertwined. "What were you up to so early this morning?" Dek asks, gently playing with her hair.

"I just got a blanket and sat out on the porch, watching the sun rise over the lake. In the morning, the lake looks like steamy glass. It's very beautiful," Lauren says. "I'm kind of a morning person, and with so much on my mind, I just couldn't sleep anymore."

"Well, you're the best kind of morning person, you know?" he says, giving her a teasing smile.

"The one who'll have morning sex with you?" she teases back.

"No," he says with a laugh. "The kind who will let a non-morning person sleep ... and then have morning sex with them." They laugh, and he gives her another long kiss. "I guess it's time to get up."

After a quick bite of some frozen breakfast sandwiches, they get to work around the house. Dek mows the yard while Lauren cleans up the house. There are a lot of dead bugs and dirt since no one's there regularly. They finish up in a few hours, then Dek runs down the street to the Wagon Wheel to get some takeout for lunch. They sit at the table on the deck, enjoying the sun and food.

"I hate to bring this up when we're having such a nice day, but we really haven't talked about it much after what happened in Chicago," Lauren starts, grabbing Dek's attention mid-bite. "What do you think about Dr. Strong's theories about what's going on with us? Do you think we could be part of the next evolutionary jump?"

Taking a minute to swallow, Dek looks out over the lake. "I guess it does kind of make sense. The changes we've been going through all seem to be related to advanced cellular functions. It's not like we're flying or punching through walls or having sound-barrier-breaking speed. We're just ... better. The next evolutionary jump should help propel a species to the next level, though not necessarily a superhuman level. If these changes occurred in everyone, just think of the ways that our society could move forward."

"I know. I was pondering the possibilities this morning over coffee. Memory, healing, and physical adaptations alone would allow for enormous advances in every science. I guess the real question is: At what cost?"

Dek turns back to Lauren. "Potentially half the human race or more," he answers solemnly. "That would make sense. With the reduction in health problems, we'd have a huge population increase if there weren't something to help make room."

"Are you ready for that? Are you?" she asks, her voice shaky and tears filling her eyes. "Are you ready to lose *half* of the world's population? I can barely cope with the four people we lost this past week."

"No, I can't imagine being responsible for something like that. I'm not sure what we should do or if we're even qualified to make such an enormous decision," Dek says before pausing when he suddenly hears movement along the side of the house.

Seemingly out of nowhere, a medium-sized, orange, fluffy dog comes walking around the house and up to them at the table.

"Hey, Koda! Way to break the tension, boy," Dek says, reaching down and petting his head. "This is Koda, the neighbor's dog. He's very friendly."

"I can see that," she says, laughing as Koda puts his front paws up on her leg.

"Hey, Dek!"

Dek looks up to see his neighbor Kim coming around the bushes down near the lakefront. He's about Dek's height and has a slim build, wearing gray cloth shorts and no shirt. Kim hates wearing shirts for whatever reason, so he's got a deep tan from hanging out at the lake every day. Kim and his wife Jane have lived next door since Dek's dad bought this place years ago. He's always been someone Dek's dad has relied on to keep an eye on the house since he's not around all the time. Kim used to be a carpenter and even helped Dek's dad build the deck. "I hope he's not botherin' y'all too much," he says with a strong Southern accent.

"Hey, Kim, not at all. This is Lauren, a friend of mine from work," Dek says, getting up and walking over to shake Kim's hand.

"Hey, Lauren, nice to meet you," Kim says with a wave. "You down here for a little vacation, Dek?" he asks, taking out a cigarette.

"Yeah, we just needed a break from work," Dek says. "The place looks good. I haven't been down here in a while."

"Your dad is down here about every other week, doing random yard work and messing around on the dock."

Dek laughs. "He loves to get away and sneak in some fishing when he gets a chance. We've got to head into town for some supplies today. Do you need anything?"

"No, we're good, just wanted to stop over and say hi. Make sure it was someone I know hangin' out over here. Can never be too careful, y'know? Y'all have a good day," Kim says before heading back around the bushes.

Dek returns to Lauren who's still petting Koda on the deck.

"He seems really nice," she says.

"He's one in a million," Dek replies as he cleans up their plates. "He goes around in his golf cart, helping people in the neighborhood when they need an extra hand." He then carries their dirty dishes inside, leaving Lauren with Koda, glad to have a break from their intense discussion from earlier. He hears his phone vibrating on the counter and instinctively answers when he sees it's James. "Hey, man, what's up?"

"'What's up'? *'What's up'*?" James repeats, clearly panicking. "Richard's *dead*, man! Wasn't he with you guys? What the fuck happened? Where are you?"

"Slow down, bud, we're fine. We did have a scare the other night, and I did hear about Richard, but he wasn't with us when it happened," Dek lies, feeling like such a shitty friend for not calling James sooner to let him know he was okay and still alive. "We got separated a while ago. I heard someone shot him?"

"Yeah. Jesus, I'm so glad to hear you're okay," James says with a sigh of relief. "By the way, your landlord called me since I'm your emergency contact and said he was trying to track you down. I think they're going to evict you if you don't call them soon.

They said it looks like you abandoned the place, and they have an interested party who'd like to rent it."

"Are you shitting me? I've been there for at least three years; they've never done anything like this before. I'm gone for a week, and this is the loyalty they show me?"

Before he can finish his thought, Lauren abruptly grabs the phone from his hand and hangs it up. "Dek, are you crazy? You can't talk on your phone! What if Vince is tracking our phones?" she yells, chucking his phone on the couch.

He stands there shocked before stammering, "I-I forgot. It was James, and I-I don't know, I just picked it up on instinct."

"These people have very good tech. The best," she says, giving him an exasperated look. "Bugs, silencers, explosives. Any of this ringing any bells? We can't take any chances. When we go to town today, we need to get new phones. I knew we should've just gotten rid of them, but I didn't get around to it yet."

"Let's just shut them off and remove the batteries," Dek suggests, retrieving and shutting down his phone.

Lauren does the same, then they lock up the house and head into Lancaster, a small town located ten minutes from the lake. They hit the local grocery store and get food, phones, and some ammunition for the hunting rifle Dek's dad keeps in the main bedroom at the lake house. Dek figures they may need some protection if Vince finds out where they're staying.

After they get back to the lake house and put everything away, they decide to get out and test Lauren's calf muscle. They spend about ten minutes stretching on the dock, letting the afternoon sun revitalize them.

"How's the leg feeling?" Dek asks, groaning as he finishes.

"I think it's almost fully healed. The swelling's down, and my flexibility's coming back," Lauren replies with a smile. "Should we take out a couple of kayaks and do some laps around the island?"

"Sounds great," Dek says before walking up the hill to get two kayaks out from under the house.

They do two laps around the island, then come to a stop on the side of the island closest to the house. They climb up the bank to the flat canopied area. The sun peeks through the leaves, casting beams of light on the floor of the island, which is covered with small seedlings and ferns not more than ten inches off the ground. The trees are massive, shooting up from the ground and disappearing in the leaves above, like giant, ancient Roman columns. The whole scene reminds Dek of a fairy hollow he saw in some children's cartoon a long time ago.

"You were right, Dek," Lauren says, her breath taken away. "This place is really cool. These giant, old trees must be at least ten feet around."

They eventually find the rusted truck and explore for a few more minutes before paddling back to the dock. There, they set up some chairs and enjoy the last sun of the evening as a bald eagle circles over the island, looking for dinner.

"Hey, Dek, do you see those two guys fishing over along the far side of the island?" Lauren asks, motioning toward their direction with a tilt of her head.

"Yeah," Dek says, trying to subtly look at the boat. "A lot of people like to fish on that side of the island because there's a drop-off in the water's depth. I noticed them earlier, but I didn't see anything suspicious."

"Do you think they're looking for us?" Lauren asks, taking his hand.

"I do," he replies, trying to hide a smirk. "Us and that mythical giant catfish people claim they've seen around here." He's hoping a little humor might lighten her mood, but she just gives him a you're-not-funny glare. He clears his throat and decides to change the subject. "Let's go up and get a bite to eat. Leave the kayaks down by the water. We may go out again in the morning when the water's calmer."

"Yeah, all right … I guess I'm overreacting a bit," Lauren says as they head inside, glancing over her shoulder for one last glimpse.

***

The two fishermen return to the public boat launch a few miles up the river just before dusk and pull their boat out of the water. A man in a truck is waiting for them to pull out so he can put in his twelve-foot fishing boat.

As the fishermen tie down their boat for the drive home, they watch the man in the truck line up his boat on the ramp. He has long, scraggy, white hair and a white beard. One of the fishermen offers to help the old-timer, only to be waved off as the man slips the boat off his trailer into the water with the ease of a seasoned pro. He then pulls his truck forward and walks back toward his boat, carrying a large duffle bag.

"Hey, fella!" one of the fishermen yells from their car. "Might not be the best time for night fishing. Looks like a storm might be coming in."

The man ignores them and gets in his boat, pulling out into the river and traveling south toward Fishing Creek Lake. After about a mile, the man pulls over near the shore and gets out a fishing pole set up with a bobber and hook but no bait. He casts in his line and sets his pole nose-up in the boat.

After casually glancing around the river to make certain he's alone, Mr. Vincent pulls off his fake beard and wig and lays them in the water over the side of the boat. He puts on a black baseball hat and checks his GPS. It's only a ten-minute ride down the river to the last cell phone coordinates for Mr. Thomas's phone. Giving a call to Thomas's friend, Mr. Stratman, and pretending to be the landlord paid off big time. Any true friend would want to give a heads-up about something like that.

Looking up, Mr. Vincent notices the two fishermen at the boat launch were correct; it does look like rain will be blowing in shortly. Good. That should give some extra cover. He opens the duffle bag at his feet and checks his supplies—two silenced Berettas, night vision goggles, a scoped rifle, and a small explosive package that could be used to simulate an electrical fire. That should destroy any evidence of him having been there; these old lake houses burn down due to faulty wiring all the time. He leans back in the boat's chair and checks his watch. Ten minutes until sunset, another thirty minutes for total darkness.

It's been a while since he's had a challenging case like this one. He's mainly been working in the private sector for the last four years. Cleaning up an overdosed hooker in a CEO's hotel room or handling a corporate whistleblower was most of the action he'd seen before Helms brought him in for this deal. During Mr. Vincent's time as a contractor in Iraq, he was challenged daily. Just his Caucasian skin alone marked him as an outsider. He bartered for information in a world that worked against him; every lead had to be vetted, and behind every door was someone who hated him and wanted him gone. It's obviously not the same, chasing two young kids around the US, but the frustration they've continued to heap upon him reminds him of those old days. Even though they seem to be utterly unaware he's hot on their tail or of his main objective, they do just enough to surprise him and get away every time. However, in the next hour and a half, all that is going to change.

He picks up his pole and appears to be monitoring his bobber, but a dark smile creeps across his face. He's going to take great pleasure in his work tonight. Although he tries to avoid it, this job has become personal.

CHAPTER 32

After having a nice dinner outside, Dek and Lauren make their way to the couch in the front room and watch a storm come in. "I think the rain should start just after sunset," Dek says, looking up the weather radar on his new cell phone.

"I love just sitting here, looking out over the lake. It's very peaceful out here," Lauren says, leaning her head against his shoulder.

He sets his phone down on the table next to the couch and takes her hand. "What do you think we should do about all this craziness we've been caught up in?"

After thinking for a moment, Lauren sits up and turns toward him. "I think we have to go to the police. We need to expose Helms Chemical for what they're doing. The lives that have been lost can't have been for nothing."

Dek can see the hurt in her eyes as she remembers the friends they've lost over the last few days. "I agree. Let's go to the police and probably the news media as well. To what extent should we tell them about the accident and what it's done to us?" he asks. Before she can answer, he continues, panicking slightly, "I'm afraid we could be carrying a very dangerous virus. We could be contagious. We could be deemed a public threat and put into isolation. I know we need to go to the police to expose the bad guys, but should we expose ourselves in the process?"

"Dek," she says calmly, "I think we have to. If any of that is true, and we find out later that we harmed a lot of innocent people, I don't think we could live with ourselves. You saw how the cells in the experiment reacted to sunlight after being infected by the virus. Some were fine, but what happened to the others could be catastrophic."

They look up when a flash of lightning suddenly strikes the earth off in the distance. It's followed a few seconds later with a clap of thunder.

"It's getting dark. Do you want to look through the old DVDs and see if we can find a movie to watch?" he asks, motioning back toward the living room. He turns on the porch light as the rain begins to fall outside. "The storm makes it pitch black out there."

Lauren goes into the kitchen to pop some popcorn and grabs two beers before plopping down on the couch. There's not a huge movie library to choose from, so Dek just picks the extended version of *The Lord of the Rings*. He puts it in the DVD player, then joins Lauren on the couch and leans over to sneak in a quick kiss as the movie starts.

About ten minutes into the movie, they hear Koda barking outside. Dek turns down the movie sound and hears Kim next door, shouting, "Come on, boy, stop all that barking! You know Mr. Decklan isn't out in this rain!" The barking stops, then Kim's door shuts as he lets Koda back inside.

As Dek raises the remote to resume the movie, Lauren grabs his hand. "I think there's someone on the deck!" she whispers urgently, eyes wide. "I just heard a board squeak, and it sounds like Koda was barking in our direction."

They're both dead quiet, listening intently. Their ears can pick up almost anything, even with all the rain. They jump to their feet when they hear another sound near the stairs leading to the upper deck. Dek grabs a flashlight off the peninsula and pulls Lauren into the back bedroom, keeping the lights off. In the closet is his dad's hunting rifle they loaded earlier when they got back from the store. He grabs it and whispers frantically, "What should we do?"

"We run!" Lauren whispers back. "If this guy's a trained killer, we don't stand a chance."

"Okay, you're right. Out the side window. Shit! I don't have the car keys. They're on the front table."

They hear movement near the front door.

"We go for the lake!" Lauren whispers. "We left the kayaks near the dock. Vince won't be expecting us to head in that direction."

Dek quickly opens the side window and quietly removes the screen. They move down toward the lake along the side of the house without detection. Once they're at the dock, they look back at the house. All the lights are still off, but with their improved vision, they can just make out a shadowy figure walking through the main living area. They give each other a frightened look as they hurriedly lower the kayaks into the water. The rain is slightly letting up as they push out and start to paddle toward the island. Their eyes adjust to the dark, but the rain and adrenaline rush still have a disorienting effect.

Just as they start to clear the dock, Dek's paddle smacks into a couple of ducks that were seeking shelter under the floating dock. They erupt from the water, startled by his paddle and squawking loudly.

"Go!" Dek yells. He reaches over, grabs Lauren's kayak, and shoves her ahead of him as hard as he can, getting her momentum up. Then they paddle like their lives depend on it. The rain cuts across their faces as the blades of their paddles plow through the water. With their enhanced strength, they're able to make the boats fly across the water. They're only about forty feet from the island when they hear the soft pops of a silenced pistol. One of the bullets shoots through the side of Dek's kayak. "Into the water!" he yells to Lauren who's about ten feet ahead of him.

She rolls her kayak, then starts swimming to shore. They hear more pops as Dek grabs the rifle and flips out of his kayak, keeping the rifle out of the water with his left hand. The overturned kayaks give them some shelter from Vince's line of sight on the dock.

"Quick, up the bank! Once we're in the trees, he won't be able to see us!" Dek hisses ahead to Lauren who's almost reached the shore. The pops have stopped for now, so he takes the opportunity to jump from the water and clamber up the bank for the trees.

More pops start the minute he comes out of the water. Dek groans in agony as a bullet hits him low on his left side. He's able to make it up the bank and finds Lauren hiding behind one of the large trees, watching the house.

"Dek, are you hurt?" she asks, running over to help him.

"Yeah," he says, putting pressure on the wound with his free hand, still clutching the rifle in the other. "I'll be fine. It just grazed my side as I was struggling to get out of the water."

They both look back when they hear a boat engine come to life near the dock. "Oh, shit! That fucker came by boat!" Dek exclaims, looking around for a place to hide.

"Wait, Dek," says Lauren, putting a hand on his arm. "You have the gun. I say we make a stand now." She looks back toward the house and can see a figure in a fishing boat slowly approaching the island near where the kayaks were abandoned. "We have the advantage. Our eyesight is near perfect in the dark."

"I don't know about that advantage," Dek says, pushing her back behind the tree. "He's probably wearing some sort of night vision goggles considering how accurate his shots were. I'll bet he can see almost as clearly as we can."

He hears the boat engine slow as it nears their position and can make out the figure in the boat. It's gotta be Vince, he's almost sure of it. Using the tree he's hiding behind for support, Dek takes aim at the man with the hunting rifle. His eyes are so sharp, he shoots the man right in the heart from fifty feet away. The man's body falls back onto the floor of the boat.

"Got him!" Dek yells, looking up from the rifle's sight. "Right in the chest."

Lauren heaves a sigh of relief, watching the boat slowly creep forward toward the shore, still slightly in gear with no one at the helm.

"Should we go check?" Dek asks, still feeling the adrenaline rushing in his body.

"I guess it's safe since you got him, right?" Lauren asks with slight hesitation.

"Definitely," he reassures her confidently.

"I still have the flashlight if we need it," she says, flipping the light into her hand.

"I think I'm better without it. Remember when we came out of the basement under the lab in Wisconsin, and the sudden light blinded our eyes? Besides, if we just shot a man, we may not want all the attention a light would bring."

The rain falls gently as they approach the boat. The engine's still running, and the man hasn't moved. The couple climb down the embankment to the edge of the water where the boat's caught on a tree branch just a few feet from the shore. Dek aims the rifle at the man in the boat, just in case. They look down and see a small pool of blood on the bottom of the boat. "I really did get him," Dek says quietly. He thinks it's Vince, but it's hard to tell because of the night vision goggles the man's wearing.

"Yep, you got him," Lauren says, pointing to the blood and bullet hole in the center of the man's fishing vest.

Dek lowers the rifle. "I've never shot a man before, but I would expect more blood than that."

Before he can say another word, Vince pops up and aims a silenced pistol right at Lauren's face. Startled, Dek tries to raise the rifle again.

"Don't move!" Vince commands, regaining his position in the boat, a maniacal smile on his face. "I do love hunting amateurs. You two have been the biggest pain in my ass, or in this case, in my chest and the back of my head," he says, rubbing the back of his head with a wince. "You idiots honestly thought I'd come out here blind and without wearing a bullet-proof vest? That was a nice shot though, and in the dark and rain even. I wasn't expecting that. Too bad I have to kill you. You'd make an excellent hitman."

"Look," Dek says, trying to buy time. For what, he isn't sure. Maybe a miracle? "You don't have to do this. We didn't tell anyone about the samples or anything that's gone down. You don't have to kill us. You can find *the light*," he adds pleading for their lives but also trying to signal Lauren.

She instantly turns her head toward him, picking up on what he's just said. "It's no use, Dek," she says solemnly. "It's over."

When Vince stiffens his grip to pull the trigger, Lauren shines the flashlight right into Vince's goggles, blinding him. He throws his hands up to shield his eyes, and she immediately dives into the water. The gun goes off, and the bullet slices through the water and her hair. Her increased speed is the only thing that saves her.

With Vince still stunned, Dek launches himself at the hitman before he can regain his composure. The men fall into the boat, and the gun gets knocked out of Vince's hand, but whatever military training he's had allows him to quickly recover. He pulls out a knife from his belt and swings it at Dek, grazing his left arm. Barely dodging the attack, Dek grabs Vince's arm and rolls them both into the cold water and moves to hold on to Vince from behind. Grasping the arm that has the knife and getting a lock around Vince's neck with his other arm, Dek quickly realizes they're sinking fast.

His first instinct is to let go and swim for the surface, but then he remembers his body has changed. He concentrates on strengthening his lungs while maintaining a firm hold on Vince as he tries to thrash free. Dek dives deeper into the black water and hears Vince's heart begin to race wildly as he realizes what Dek's planning. He claws at Dek's face with his free hand, but Dek refuses to let go.

After a few moments, the fight finally goes out of Vince, and his body goes limp. Dek releases Vince's corpse, letting it sink deeper into the dark depths of the water, then quickly swims back up to the surface.

"Dek, are you okay?" Lauren yells as he breaks through the surface of the water. She grabs him as he gasps for breath and pulls him to shore.

"I'm all right," he manages to say hoarsely after coughing up half the lake.

"Where's Vince?" she asks, searching the shoreline.

"Drowned," he says, still trying to catch his breath. "He's dead."

She looks back at him, both shocked and relieved, then throws her arms around him, almost knocking the air out of him again. "Dek, you were down there so long, I thought you both had drowned."

"I'm okay," he says, taking her face in his cold, shaky hands and kissing her. "We're going to be okay."

CHAPTER 33

Thankfully, the sound of the storm allowed the activities of the night to go unnoticed by the few houses lining the inlet. Dek and Lauren recover their things and retrieve the overturned kayaks, but they leave Vince's boat sitting in the water just off the island. Hopefully, this will be looked at as a boating accident that led to a person drowning.

When they get back to the house, Lauren gets out the first-aid kit and patches Dek up where Vince shot, cut, and scratched him. The wounds are already healing, but it's better to be safe than sorry. They decide to wait out the morning and see what happens before they get involved with the police.

**

The next day, there's a big commotion out by the island. Someone reported a boat sitting out near the island with no driver. The police come by and question everyone who lives nearby as they determine whether it was just an accident. A few days later, a body is found upriver near the dam. The damage done to the body as it traveled the five miles to the dam left the police with very little to examine.

That night, Dek and Lauren eat a quiet dinner on the deck. "It seems like it was ruled an accidental drowning," Dek says, looking for a response from Lauren. She's been very distant all day.

"I guess that's good," she says, picking at her food. "Do you think that'll be the end of it?"

"If the body traveled all the way to the dam, it's gotta be pretty beat up. I don't think they'll be able to tell how he drowned or that there was a fight," he replies.

"No, I mean, will Vince's death be the end of them chasing us, or will they just find a better person to hunt us down? We have to do something to put an end to all of this. It can't go on forever."

Dek puts down his fork and takes a deep breath. "So we turn ourselves in and tell the authorities our whole crazy story?" he half-says, half-asks. "We tell them about the accident, the virus, and what it's done to us? About the cover-up and the murders and our eventual killing of our pursuer? And we just hope that they'll understand? That they don't throw us in jail or quarantine or kill us as a potential public health risk?"

Lauren's silent for a moment, thinking about all he just pointed out. "I don't think we have a choice," she finally says. "If they're sending someone else after us, we probably won't survive another night like that. If we allow Helms Chemical to fully unleash the virus with no warning to the public, that could be catastrophic. Whatever they decide to do with us is just nominal."

"At the beginning of all this, I would've had to agree with you," Dek says, looking deep into her eyes. "I was just an empty shell, going from date to date, trying to find love, and going from day to day, trying to decide what to do with my life. Now I have a purpose. I have something to lose. Some*one* to lose. This is a big decision, and I can't deal with the idea of us being locked away like lab rats as scientists try to decide what to do with us."

Lauren leans toward him. "I was in a similar situation before we met. In the beginning, I couldn't even picture myself in another relationship, and now, I can't picture my life without you in it. I understand what you're feeling because I'm feeling it too." She pauses to wipe away a tear sliding down her cheek. "But we have to do what's right."

"This whole thing's been crazy," Dek says, reaching across the table for her hand and giving it a squeeze. "At least I found you."

She looks at him with some hope in her eyes. "I'm confident we can do the right thing ... if we do it together."

***

Once Dek has a few days to sit out on the dock and get some sun, his side and arm heal very quickly. They lock the lake house, take one last look at their temporary sanctuary, then drive into Charlotte to speak with an attorney and get some help with how to best proceed with their story. They turn into a packed parking deck and weave their way up a few flights to find a parking spot. They've spent the last few days getting organized, taking some notes, and making sure everything's ready to give to the attorney.

As they exit the car and start down the parking ramp, a black van pulls into a spot about fifty feet ahead of them, and the side door slides open. A small African American woman with a cane emerges from the far side of the van and walks slowly to the middle of the lane, stopping to face them. She's wearing worn sandals and a colorful kanga dress. Her hair is thin and gray with whips flowing down her drawn cheeks. She leans slightly forward on the brown, hardwood cane with the head of a heron bird as its handle. She can't be more than five feet tall, but she exudes an air of maturity that commands respect, and her body is radiating a very strong hum, like the man Dek and Lauren noticed in the park in Chicago but much stronger and louder.

Dek grabs Lauren by the arm and pulls them to a stop about twenty feet from the woman. They're both fixated on the woman as two men emerge from the front seats of the van who are over six feet tall and athletically built. Both are wearing jeans and black T-shirts, and they casually walk to either side of the woman, standing about two feet behind her.

Dek feels like he's seen them before. He suddenly remembers and says, "The cop from the motel!" At the same time Lauren says, "That's the homeless man from Madison!" They turn back, planning to bolt for their car.

"Stop!" the small woman yells with a crackling voice, staring at them from between the two men.

Dek glances at Lauren as they're both paralyzed, unable to move anything but their eyes. The hum emanating from the woman has increased and is almost deafening. They exchange a look of panic as the two men move to stand on either side of them. "I love working with her," says the cop. Dek and Lauren turn their eyes from the men to the old woman in front of them.

"Did you really think you were the only two people on Earth to be affected by the virus?" she asks quietly, leaning forward on her cane and raising her eyebrows. "Sleep."

Then they collapse into the waiting arms of the two men.

EPILOGUE

In a large office building near the center of Quito, one of the biggest cities in Ecuador, Mr. Feldman is exiting an elevator on the sixteenth floor. With his thin build and long gait, he looks like a giraffe loping through the office space, carrying only a black briefcase. He passes through a maze of workers in cubicles who are busily typing away or answering phones that never stop ringing. He arrives at a secure door near the back of the room, then heads down another small hallway, entering a windowless boardroom. The room has a large center table lined with comfy, leather office chairs. Mr. Helms is seated at the far end of the table with a laptop in front of him, and a female secretary detail is standing off to his right, finishing up a dictation.

"Ah, there you are, Feldman," Mr. Helms booms. "Lizbeth, please excuse us. We have a private matter to discuss. I'll call you back in when we're done."

After Lizbeth nods and leaves the room, Feldman takes a seat next to Helms, setting his briefcase on the table.

"Any news on the situation in the Carolinas?" Helms asks, glancing up from his laptop.

"Mr. Vincent was found dead in a lake in South Carolina about an hour south of Charlotte. He didn't have anything on his person, his boat, or his car that would lead anyone to us. There's also no sign of Thomas and Summers. They seem to have dropped off the face of the Earth. Thomas's father owns a small house on the lake where Mr. Vincent was found. We sent someone down there to check, but they're not there. I can only believe they're hiding out, maybe worried they had something to do with Mr. Vincent's death. The police are calling it an 'accidental drowning' at this point, and that's a best-case scenario for us."

Helms closes his laptop. "So, you're telling me that two twenty-something scientists with no espionage experience have somehow been able to drop off the grid?" He shakes his head and leans back in his chair. "Someone must be helping them. Mr. Vincent was fine with taking care of simple tasks and keeping things quiet, but it sounds like this one was too much for him. I think that we have to call in that European group we used in the Middle East. If Thomas and Summers go to the police or the press, this whole project could go up in smoke."

"At least they're keeping quiet for now. I'll contact the Heretic Group and have them send out a team," Feldman reassures him. He then reaches into his briefcase and pulls out a small white package, placing it on the table. "We received this package from Mr. Vincent yesterday. It appears he was successful in retrieving the missing filter from the Madison lab."

"Well, I guess he managed to do one thing right," Helms replies coldly, sliding the package across the table to the side of his laptop. "When do we begin the extraction of the technetium?"

"All of the mining rights have been signed over. The first and second shipments of mining equipment arrived earlier this week and should be at dig site one by Monday. The engineer in charge of the dig is still skeptical about the possibility of removing a significant amount of technetium with mining alone. He's ordered in some explosives as a backup plan."

"Good, very good," Helms says with a satisfied smile. "That unique radiation signature will be a key component as this company evolves from Helms Chemical to Helms Terminal Guidance systems."

Printed in the USA
CPSIA information can be obtained
at www.ICGtesting.com
CBHW030956230324
5757CB00011B/620